A Most Diabolical Plot

Six compelling Sherlock Holmes cases

By Tim Symonds

Paperback: 978-1-78705-404-2
ePub: 978-1-78705-405-9
PDF: 978-1-78705-406-6

Published in the UK by MX Publishing
335 Princess Park Manor, Royal Drive, London, N11 3GX
www.mxpublishing.com

Cover by Brian Belanger zhahadun@myfairpoint.net

Tim Symonds was born in London. He grew up in Somerset, Dorset and the British Crown Dependency of Guernsey. After several years travelling widely, including farming on the slopes of Mt. Kenya and working on the Zambezi River in Central Africa, he emigrated to the United States. He studied at Göttingen, in Germany, and the University of California, Los Angeles, graduating Phi Beta Kappa.

Tim Symonds at Nagarkot Hill Station Himalayas

He is a Fellow of the Royal Geographical Society.

Detective novels by the author include - *Sherlock Holmes And The Mystery Of Einstein's Daughter, Sherlock Holmes And The Case Of The Bulgarian Codex, Sherlock Holmes And The Dead Boer At Scotney Castle, Sherlock Holmes And The Sword Of Osman*, and *Sherlock Holmes And The Nine-Dragon Sigil.*

Website http://tim-symonds.co.uk/

To my ever-beautiful partner-in-crime Lesley Abdela

Contents

A Most Diabolical Plot

by Tim Symonds

From the Notebooks of Dr. John H. Watson MD, late of the Indian Army

Not 'til the Last Day, when the bugle blows for me, shall I forget the most diabolical attempt ever made on my friend Sherlock Holmes's life. We were in the autumn of 1903. My wife was away, and I was once more in the airy living-room of the lodgings I had shared with Holmes on the first floor of 221, Baker Street. Our landlady Mrs. Hudson came in with my breakfast, together with the morning edition of the *Westminster Gazette*. The newspaper contained a selection of the year's significant events to date – on February 3rd a British expedition captured the mud-walled city of Kano. Under Pelham Warner's captaincy, the first cricket tour of Australia was in its final planning stages. I was about to turn my attention to the plate of kidneys, kedgeree and ham when my eye was caught by a short article on an inside page titled 'Mystery Disappearance of Society Murderer'.

> *Nothing has been seen of Colonel Sebastian Moran, formerly 1st Bangalore Pioneers and well-known at London's card-playing clubs, since his unpublicised release from Newgate last year when the gaol was closed for demolition. The Colonel served only half of a twenty-year sentence for the wilful murder of his gambling partner, the Honourable Ronald Adair, second son of the Earl of Maynooth. Moran fell into a trap laid by Inspector Lestrade of Scotland Yard less than a decade ago when the former attempted to assassinate the famous Consulting Detective Sherlock Holmes, employing an ingenious air-gun designed to shoot bullets instead of lead pellets. To gain early release, Colonel Moran vowed to turn his considerable talents to good causes.*

6

I lowered the newspaper and stared unseeing at the wall. More than forty determined attempts had been made upon Holmes's life in the twenty-plus years since we had taken up lodgings together, yet I recalled in exact detail Moran's failure in 1894, which led to his arrest and imprisonment. It was preceded by the murder mentioned, taking place in unusual and inexplicable circumstances. At the time, Holmes remarked, "That had all the hallmarks of Colonel Moran." He reached up to a bookshelf for his Index of biographies, adding, "My collection of M's is a fine one. Morgan the poisoner, and Merridew of abominable memory, and Mathews, who knocked out my left canine in the waiting-room at Charing Cross. And, finally, here is our friend."

He passed the Index to me.

> MORAN, SEBASTIAN, COLONEL. Born London, 1840. Son of Sir Augustus Moran, C.B., once British Minister to Persia. Educated Eton and Oxford. Served in Jowaki Campaign, Afghan Campaign, Charasiab (despatches), Sherpur, and Cabul. Address: Conduit Street. Clubs: The Anglo-Indian, the Tankerville, the Bagatelle Card Club. Recruited by the 'Napoleon of Crime', Professor Moriarty, serving as his Chief of Staff, but used solely for assassinations that require rare skill with the rifle.

Scratched in the margins in Holmes's precise hand were the words, *The second most dangerous man in London'*.

"As you have a fountain pen in your hand, Watson, please update the entry," Holmes had requested. "Now the Napoleon of Crime Moriarty is dead, could you strike out 'second' as in 'The *second* most dangerous man in London'? Moran has inherited the rank as our principal foe."

Once Moran had been safely tucked away in Newgate Prison, I gave him less thought throughout the years than to the industrious navigators repairing the canals of Mars. It came as a nasty shock to learn of his release. I assumed the murderer would stay locked up for many years to come. I folded the *Gazette* and cast a glance across the back garden to a wall giving access into Siddons Lane. More than once, in fear of attack from Baker Street itself, Holmes and I achieved a quick exit by that back route. I made a mental note to inform my comrade that Moran was on the loose, turning to my writing-desk to put the final touches to our most recent case for submission to *The Strand Magazine*.

Within the hour the manuscript was finished. I threw down the pen and looked out of the window. A warm, lazy summer lay behind us, the third since Edward VII assumed the throne of England. I could spend a leisurely hour in nearby Regents Park watching the herons' antics on their tiny island before strolling on to *The Strand's* offices on Southampton Street. The Art Editor would commission a few simple line drawings from the well-known artist Mr. Sidney Paget to illustrate the story. With luck, it would be picked up across the Atlantic by the editor of *Collier's* magazine.

The grandfather clock struck the hour. Holmes came up the stairs at his customary three-at-a-time. On most days, as he had that day, he left the flat before daybreak for London's East End, forever observing the rapacious ivory-traders and dragsmen in the welter of streets in Stepney and Whitechapel. On other days, he journeyed down to the English county of Sussex to oversee the construction of dew ponds on the isolated bee-farm he had recently purchased.

My comrade's head appeared around the door, a Coutts cheque flapping in his hand.

He said in a most affable tone, "Courtesy of the mid-day post, the Duchess of Burwash has at last settled her account. Name any restaurant in the whole of England and allow me to invite you to dine there this weekend – I have obligations until then. What do you say to a fish-dinner? Shall we take a scow along the river to *The Ship* in Greenwich?"

The invitation came as a welcome surprise. When fortune smiles I am prepared to lay out two days' Army pension on partridge or an over-ripe pheasant at one of my clubs, or, for a special treat, Rother Rabbit with broccoli, followed by Lady Pettus' biscakes. Holmes, by contrast, even when he is the honoured guest of a wealthy client, has been known to call for a tin of his favourite over-salted Benitez corned beef.

"Holmes, I accept this rare invitation," I replied, adding emphatically, "with alacrity."

"And your choice of restaurant for our celebratory meal?" Holmes asked.

"If you really do mean any restaurant in the whole of England, I shall opt for Simpson's Grand Cigar Divan."

"A fine decision," Holmes acknowledged cheerily.

I saw he was settling in for the day at a particularly noxious chemical experiment. I took my hat and strolled to the heronry in Regents Park, followed by a two mile walk to deliver the manuscript to my publishers.

The weekend approached. I stood at the sitting-room window, staring down at the bustling street. A diligence pulled by a team of Boulonnais mares was commencing its long journey, destination Glasgow and Scotland's ports to the Western Isles. The invaluable little Street Arabs known to Holmes and me as the Baker Street Irregulars bowled home-made hoops along the paving. Their ragged gang-leader, young Simpson, ran to the diligence's side, begging for a coin or fruit from well-dressed passengers. A tall figure was ambling towards our front-door in a collarless cotton shirt and corduroy trousers, sporting a high, soft hat with a pipe stuck in the side of it, and a waistcoat reaching down almost to his knees. It was Holmes in a disguise new to me. With a quick sideways dart he came in.

The morning post had come and gone without intrusion into our world, but a rat-tat-tat at the front door a few minutes later indicated a special delivery. Mrs. Hudson came up the stairs with a letter for Holmes. He read it and was about to place it in his notebook when he caught sight of my expectant face. He tossed the page across with a laugh.

Unusually, the letter was from Inspector Lestrade, the Scotland Yard policeman Holmes first encountered in a case years before.

Lestrade's note read:

Dear Mr. Holmes,

I'm told you've been hanging around the London Docks disguised as a common Irish labourer. I wonder what mischief you're getting up to now? When you've settled back in your digs and have a moment to spare, we at the Yard would appreciate your cooperation in a pretty little mystery. Please give our cordial good wishes to Dr. Watson.

G. Lestrade.

There was a lengthy postscript.

I almost forgot. You will by now have seen the news your friend Colonel Sebastian Moran was released from Newgate Prison. So far, he seems to be conforming to the terms of good behaviour for obtaining his freedom early. There has been no sign of him at the Anglo-Indian, the Bagatelle Card Club, or the Tankerville. We believe we've traced him to a lonely and isolated farmhouse on the Haddiscoe Marshes, on the borders of Suffolk and Essex. An elderly man described as thin, with a projecting nose, high bald forehead, cruel blue eyes, and a huge grizzled moustache, has taken a short lease on the place, near some abandoned Maltings. He sports a red and black silk cravat, Moran's old neckwear. Superstition, no doubt. Magical thinking gives half the world's criminals away. The man surrounds his land in every direction with DANGER KEEP OUT signs. He may not plan to stay there for long. According to the village woman who "does" for him, the house is only sparsely furnished. He has a pair of commonplace ceramic dogs, a postcard of the Sussex cricketer, K.S. Ranjitsinhji, on the mantelpiece, a few pieces of old-fashioned china, and a couple of rickety chairs.

I read in Police Review *you have bought a farm in Sussex and are the owner of several hives of bees, with plans to write an opus on the meadow-flower in Mesolithic honey cultures. By a strange coincidence, Moran's taken up bee-keeping himself. The postman reported several deliveries of bees, though not the patriotic British bee. The Colonel's bees arrived from East Africa. What's odd is the way he's housing them. Instead of proper wooden-frame hives, he had an old skepper make up the baskets from coils of grass with a single entrance at the bottom, the way my grandfather used to. I say "odd," because I'm told these skeps have serious disadvantages compared to proper hives. Skeps are lighter in weight and easier to transport, but you can't inspect the comb for pests and diseases, and you may have to destroy the bee colony (and the skep) to remove the honey.*

I was relieved by the information that Moran, formerly so obsessed with seeking Holmes's death, had been tracked to a lair on the border of Suffolk and Essex, a good distance from Holmes's own isolated bee-farm on the Sussex Downs.

Moran's capture and imprisonment and our part in it flooded back. It took place at midnight in an empty house across the street from our lodgings, a setting with an unhampered view of our sitting-room. Moran planned to shoot Holmes through our window with the same remarkable

11

weapon he used to murder his former whist partner, the Honourable Ronald Adair. Unfortunately for Moran, Holmes was one step ahead of him.

I can do no better than to repeat my description in 'The Adventure of the Empty House':

> *A low, stealthy sound came to my ears, not from the direction of Baker Street, but from the back of the very house in which we lay concealed. A door opened and shut. An instant later steps crept down the passage-steps which were meant to be silent, but which reverberated harshly through the empty house. Holmes crouched back against the wall, and I did the same, my hand closing upon the handle of my revolver.*
>
> *Peering through the gloom, I saw the vague outline of a man, a shade blacker than the blackness of the open door. He stood for an instant, and then he crept forward, crouching, menacing, into the room. He was within three yards of us, this sinister figure, and I had braced myself to meet his spring, before I realized that he had no idea of our presence. He passed close beside us, stole over to the window, and softly and noiselessly raised it for half a foot. As he sank to the level of this opening, the light of the street, no longer dimmed by the dusty glass, fell full upon his face.*
>
> *The man seemed to be beside himself with excitement. His eyes shone like stars, and his features were working convulsively. An opera hat was pushed to the back of his head, and an evening dress shirt-front gleamed out through his open overcoat. His face was gaunt and swarthy, scored with deep, savage lines. In his hand he carried what appeared to be a stick, but as he laid it down upon the floor it gave a metallic clang. Then from the pocket of his overcoat he drew a bulky object, and he busied himself in some task which ended with a loud, sharp click, as if a spring or bolt had fallen into its place.*
>
> *Still kneeling upon the floor he bent forward and threw all his weight and strength upon some lever, with the result that there*

came a long, whirling, grinding noise, ending once more in a powerful click. He straightened himself then, and I saw that what he held in his hand was a sort of gun, with a curiously misshapen butt. He opened it at the breech, put something in, and snapped the breech-lock. I heard a little sigh of satisfaction as he cuddled the butt into his shoulder. For an instant he was rigid and motionless. Then his finger tightened on the trigger.

There was a strange, loud whiz and a long, silvery tinkle of broken glass across the street. At that instant Holmes sprang like a tiger on to the marksman's back, and hurled him flat upon his face. The man was up again in a moment, and with convulsive strength seized Holmes by the throat, but I struck him on the head with the butt of my revolver, and he dropped again upon the floor. There was the clatter of running feet upon the pavement, and two policemen in uniform, with one plain-clothes detective, rushed through the front entrance and into the room. Moran's eyes fixed upon Holmes's face with an expression in which hatred and amazement were equally blended. "You fiend!" he kept on muttering. "You clever, clever fiend!" – adding, "I shall break free from gaol, I can assure you, Holmes. And then I shall come and get you."

The evening arrived for the 'Duchess' celebratory meal at Simpson's Grand Cigar Divan. The head waiter led us to a table overlooking the Strand. We ordered sherry at an extravagant 1/- the glass. Over the years, famous authors and politicians had sat at the same table, including William Gladstone. Each Feast of All Souls, Charles Dickens booked this same table with fellow members of the Everlasting Club to discuss the occult, Egyptian magic, and second sight.

The window commanded a fine sweep of the Adelphi Theatre. I felt satisfaction as I watched a line of velvet-gowned women and tail-coated men awaiting entry to see my new play. A case of ours had been adapted as a popular piece. One theatre critic said, "*All London shivers ….*" *The Sunday Times* pronounced, *"A Corker! The audience was spellbound. Dr. John Watson's delightful play raises questions which should rally and startle all sincere students of the deductive arts."*

We commenced our meal with a white soup of chicken, almonds, and lashings of cream, and waited for the main course. After a suitable time, the Chef appeared. Walking behind him was a lesser mortal pushing a silver dinner wagon. The Chef served Holmes's slices of beef with a heavy portion of fat, carved from a large, succulent joint. I opted for the smoked salmon at a price well beyond my own pocket. For dessert, we chose the treacle sponge, with a dressing of Madagascan vanilla custard.

Holmes's mood became pensive. I enquired why. With a wistful look, he replied, "I rather hope Colonel Moran won't keep the promises he made to gain his early release. I missed matching my wits against him while he was locked away. I quite like it when he gets up to his tricks. Some definite villainy in the blood passes down in his ancestry. From the point of view of the criminal expert, England has become a singularly uninteresting country since the extinction of his boss, the most dangerous and capable criminal in Europe. While Professor Moriarty was in the field, every morning my gazette presented infinite possibilities."

When Moriarty had been "in the field," Holmes had described him without a hint of hyperbole as "the organizer of half that is evil and nearly all that is undetected in this great city. He is a genius, a philosopher, an abstract thinker."

I threw down my napkin with an incredulous smile.

"Holmes, my dear chap! Surely you don't suffer from a lack of excitement? Almost weekly we catch the froufrou of Cabinet Ministers' and political dukes' frock-coats as they clamber up our stairs to seek your assistance. Why, take our most recent case …."

"Watson," came the wry reply, "the crisis once over, the actors pass out of our lives forever. I value your effort to console me with my notoriety, but I insist that every morning one must win a victory and every evening we must fight the good fight to retain our place, or else I must seek early retirement."

I was about to console him further with, "I have no doubt that very soon Inspector Lestrade will bang on our door to summon us to the scene of another baffling crime," when we became aware a small tureen had appeared on our table, sitting apart from the magnificent silverware. I summoned the waiter. No, he replied. Absolutely not. He knew nothing about it.

Holmes pulled the vessel towards him and cautiously raised the lid. Inside lay an envelope marked 'Sherlock Holmes, Esq.'. He flicked it to me. It contained a single sheet of Trafalgar blue note-paper upon which, in a scribbled hand, were written the words:

Dear Holmes, I know you will welcome me back into the world of the living. I have given considerable thought to the person who put me in Dante's Inferno (Seventh Circle) in the first place. I do not wish to put that person to great inconvenience but I wonder if he and I might arrange an encounter?

My heart missed a beat. I had no need to read the initials at the bottom of the note. It was from the viperous Colonel Sebastian Moran, once the right-hand man of Professor Moriarty whose criminal network had stretched from the Bentinck Street corner of Welbeck Street to the Daubensee above the Gemmi Pass.

Moran's letter was a reminder how often he had sought revenge for the death of his erstwhile Paymaster.

He continued, *'It's been far too long since we met and decided certain things. Three years before I was consigned to gaol you thwarted me on the 4th and 23rd of January. Two years before my incarceration, you thwarted me in the middle of February. In my last year of freedom you were good enough to wait until the end of March. You will understand why I felt it necessary to launch an attack on you. For too long, Professor*

15

Moriarty allowed you, through your continual persecution, to place him in positive danger of losing life or liberty, with results we know well.'

Wittily, Moran penned, *'Your compulsive urge to interfere in my life presents a hereditary tendency of the most diabolical kind.'*

Holmes had sent Professor Moriarty plummeting to his doom in the Reichenbach Falls. With a deliberate reference to the rushing waters, Moran went on, *'Given our mutual interest in cascades, I suggest we get together at the Old Roar Waterfall above Hastings, conveniently near your bee-farm in Sussex. I have looked in my memorandum-book for a date. Shall we say around two o'clock on the afternoon of the first Monday of the coming month? I shall await your attendance for the final discussion of those questions which formerly lay between you and Professor Moriarty, which now, in his enforced absence, lie between you and me.'*

The Colonel signed off with a sardonic *'Pray give my greetings to your Sancho Panza, Dr. Watson. The Doctor and his antique Service revolver will be most welcome to join us.'*

The jibes were followed with an impudent, *'Believe me to be, my dear chap, very sincerely yours, S.M.'*

I folded Moran's letter. A murderous rage took control of my senses. Colonel, I thought, this time you will meet your quietus. My comrade, or better still his Sancho Panza, shall rid this world of you once and for all.

The rage subsided. Soon Holmes and I would be seated in a train on our way to Hastings, my trusty Service revolver in a pocket, a great adventure in the air. My heart began to sing. The Old Roar Waterfall it shall be – on the first Monday of the coming month!

A reflective note is in order here. Over the years I have come to realise the gods (more so the goddesses) play a remarkable role in our lives. During my military service in our Indian possessions, I often heard and repeated the word *kismet* in Urdu and Hindi, interpreted as *Fate* or *Providence*. Three 'ifs', both providential and fateful, led to my years as Sherlock

Holmes's chronicler, the happiest and most fulfilling decades of my life. First, if the doctor in the village of my upbringing had not regaled me with stories of his time as a field surgeon in the Eastern War, serving with French and British armies at Sevastopol, I may never have had the ambition to become an Army doctor myself. Second, if a ricocheting bullet from a hostile Afghan tribesman had missed me by an inch rather than thudding into my flesh (to stay there the rest of my life,) whereupon the Army left me, I would have served out my time on The Grim rather than being forced to return to England with hardly more than a wound-stripe and a pile of Service chevrons to my name. And thirdly, if I had had any family members in England other than a dissolute brother, I may not have found myself alone in London in 1881 in urgent need of diggings. In which case I would never have mentioned my search for accommodation to Stamford, my old dresser from Barts Hospital. He introduced me that same day to a young man also in need of bachelors' quarters, bearing the unusual Old English Christian name of *Sherlock*.

Now, all these years later, a further 'If' was about to intervene.

The first Monday of the month approached. My 'antique' Service revolver was oiled and ready. Holmes and I planned our trek in every detail. Old Roar Waterfall was known to me only through a sketch a century earlier by the landscape painter, J.M.W. Turner, now at the Tate Gallery. The chalk and graphite depiction portrayed a wild gully set in a deeply cut, narrow, wooded valley above the isolated fishing village of Hastings. The gully enjoyed the clime and dense plant life of a tropical jungle, home to rare orchids, bird and insect species. There was only one path to the falls, through terrain ideal for an ambuscade. Our foe Moran, as author of *Heavy Game of the Western Himalayas* and *Three Months in the Jungle*, was no stranger to ambuscades. A hunter of iron nerve, he had once crawled down a drain after a wounded man-eating tiger.

Perhaps because we faced the possibility of death at the hands of a merciless assassin, there was considerable jocularity between Holmes and me as we discussed our plans. In 'The Adventure of the Empty House', Holmes lured the Colonel to his capture and incarceration by substituting himself with a remarkably life-like wax effigy, executed by Monsieur Oscar Meunier of Grenoble. The bust was placed in full view in our Baker Street window. Once in every quarter of an hour, our obliging landlady crawled in below window level to twist and turn the figure. Holmes now proposed I borrow the full-size wax figure of himself from Madame Tussaud's to place like a ventriloquist's dummy among the orchids and ferns at Old Roar Waterfall. The wax figure and I would sit where Turner sat, squatting up to our nostrils in ferns. I could, Holmes suggested, for the sake of *auld lang syne*, wear my 'Shikar', a favourite solar topee purchased at the Army & Navy Stores at a hefty 13/6d.

Holmes didn't laugh often, but when he did it boded ill for a foe. After we had done chuckling, we turned our attention to the serious matter at hand. The Colonel would apply the expertise gained in his years hunting the Bengal tiger. He would carve out a *machan* among the ferns, mosses, and liverworts of the wet dead wood to pick us off before we as much as caught sight of him. We planned to play him at his own game – construct our own machans ahead of him and wait silently for our human tiger through the night and into the following morning.

The stakes were high. Moran notoriously never played by the Englishman's unspoken rule of giving the other side a sporting chance. This time, neither would we. We would follow the diktat of natural justice. Soon Colonel Sebastian Moran would trouble us or this world no more.

So engrossed were we with our preparations that it did not strike us for an instant that Moran's challenge was a hoodwink. The stinging use of Sancho Panza, rather than chronicler, even *amanuensis*, had made my blood boil. Ditto the deliberate mockery of my trusty Service revolver. There was the goading tone, the almost nostalgic choice of setting, echoing the far mightier, more majestic Reichenbach in the Swiss Alps. But as it transpired, Moran had no intention of facing us at Old Roar Waterfall. He was putting in place a plan as devilish as human wit could devise.

When Lestrade of the Yard apprised us of Sebastian Moran's hideaway, he mentioned *en passant* how the Colonel had taken up raising bees. I dismissed this curious fact as mere coincidence and forgot all about it. *Kismet* was once more to intervene. If I had not retreated to a comfortable arm-chair after a decent lunch and a bottle of Albariño at the Junior United Service Club…

I left the Club's handsome dining-room for the reading-room and was drifting into a nap behind a copy of *The Times* when an apparition from my long-gone days in Afghanistan appeared at my elbow.

"Why, it's Watson, isn't it?" a voice exclaimed. "Blow me down! Do you recognise me?"

For a moment I struggled to determine whether the figure was real or a figment of a reverie until he leaned forward and clapped me on the shoulder. How could I forget! Surgeon-Major Alexander Preston had been with me in the thick of the Battle of Maiwand. His experience, gained through an earlier stint in The Crimea, served the Regiment well. Throughout the battle he bore himself with the traditional nonchalance of a British surgeon in a tight place, while all around our men were going down to a humiliating defeat.

Preston explained he was in London just for a day or two, restocking his supply of medicines. We reminisced about old times. He recounted the events after I was wounded and removed from the field. Ayub Khan's officer corps had been strengthened by the large number of Sepoys who fled to his side after the failure of the Indian Rebellion. Nevertheless, Preston sensed the enemy was losing morale despite their superior numbers, until the day was saved for Ayub by a young woman by the name of Malalai. Alarmed by her side's mounting despair, she seized the Afghan flag and shouted: *"Young love! If you do not fall in the battle of Maiwand, by God, someone is saving you as a symbol of shame!"* Her cry rallied the Pashtuns to victory.

We reminisced further for a good while before I turned to the present and asked Preston where he was now practicing medicine.

"You say you're in London only briefly," I said. "Which means what? Where do you live now?"

Using the Sanskrit for the Hindu Kush, he replied, "Not in the *Pāriyātra Parvata*, I can tell you! I'm in the deepest English countryside. Miles from anywhere. After my time in Army Medical Service, life in the most primitive village in England suits me completely. A few cottages huddled around the tiny church of the Blessed Virgin and St. John the Baptist. No telegraph office. Just the one telephone, at the Railway Arms. Not much else. I deliver a few peasant women's babies, treat the occasional marsh fever, even take out an appendix once in a while. The quietest place you can imagine."

The Surgeon-Major paused.

"Mark you, something did happen only a few days ago...never seen anything like it. There's nothing in the medical records nor anything on apiculture that I can find."

I raised my eyebrows.

"Apiculture?" I queried.

"Yes, bees, hives, that sort of thing."

"I know the word," I returned, "but what has that to do with your medical practice?"

He recounted how two sturdy walkers had decided to trek across remote marshes three or four miles from his surgery. They ignored the 'Keep Out' boards, holding that signs in the countryside did not apply to visitors from London.

"Then something very curious and inexplicable took place, Watson," Preston continued. "The hikers were passing a cluster of abandoned Maltings when a witness said a swarm of bees poured out like a sudden dark rain-cloud. Most bees are quite polite if you don't disturb their nests. They don't usually chase you for over half a mile if you're rushing away as fast as your legs can take you. These bees did. Their ferocity was terrible. They attacked the two poor blighters relentlessly. In appearance, there was nothing exceptional about the bees. Possibly they were even slightly smaller than our familiar black honeybee. I estimate they inflicted two thousand stings on each of their victims. A bee stinger is barbed, like a harpoon. When you consider a human can die with just a hundred stings..."

My narrator threw up his hands.

"By the time the local farmer came to fetch me, there was nothing I could do. Both men died within minutes."

He added, "The owner of the skeps must have worried the authorities would bring a charge of criminal negligence against him – as they should. That same night he upped sticks and disappeared, taking his bees with him."

I sprang to my feet.

"Tell me, Preston," I demanded, "where exactly do you have your practice? You say deepest countryside. Did this by any chance take place along the Stour, near a village by the name of Haddiscoe?"

My old Army comrade looked stunned.

"Why, my old friend!" he exclaimed, "you seem to have developed psychic powers! Heavens above, you'll be excreting ectoplasm next. That's exactly where the incident took place."

My blood chilled. All was now clear. The invitation to a showdown at the Old Roar Waterfall was a red herring, designed to engineer Holmes's absence from his orderly rows of hives. From his Stour Valley remoteness our enemy had hatched the most cunning, deadly plot ever devised against us. While we crept our way through the undergrowth to the waterfall, Moran would be on the Downs preparing a deadly trap for us. He would switch Holmes's tractable *apis mellifera mellifera*, at home in Britain since the last Ice Age, for the breed of hideously dangerous African bees which stung the unfortunate London visitors to death. Holmes was known to walk between his rows of hives without veil or gloves. The moment we returned from our futile trek to the waterfall, we would suffer the same fate as the hikers on the Suffolk marshes. The postcard of the Sussex cricketer K.S. Ranjitsinhji in Moran's rented farmhouse indicated Moran had already reconnoitred the area. At this very moment, he and his deadly skeps might be within striking distance of Holmes's own bee-yard, tucked away in secondary woodland which had quickly recolonized my comrade's sheep-free land. I bid a rapid goodbye to my Regimental friend and hurried off to find a telephone, muttering to myself on the way, "Moran, you cunning, cunning fiend!"

Inspector Lestrade was often out of his depth and chronically lacked imagination, but on this occasion he became a man of action and authority. He pointed out that Moran would have his henchmen watching our every move. The Colonel would unfold his plot only if he was assured we were well away from the bee-farm. One glimpse of our presence on Holmes's bee-farm on the day and the effort to catch Moran *in flagrante delicto* and kill or return him to gaol would fail. Lestrade ordered us to continue with our established plan. He telegraphed Tobias Gregson, the policeman who was keeping an eye on Holmes's bee-farm, to ask him to make rapid enquiries. Gregson replied the same day. Mysterious lights, more often seen over graveyards, had been spotted at Holmes's

Hodcombe Farm, resulting in rumours of will-o'-the-wisps. Locals were giving the spot a wide berth.

By now the deadly skeps would be on their wooden bases for ease of transport, the entrances filled with loose grass to allow the bees to breath but prevent their exit. Reluctantly, we agreed to make our way to Old Roar Waterfall.

Our departure for Hastings should be as conspicuous as possible. In the meantime, Lestrade, Gregson, and a dozen armed police set up their ambuscade. They would lie in wait on the Downs. If Moran surrendered, our foe would be returned to gaol to serve out the remainder of his sentence. If he resisted...every one of Lestrade's squad was a marksman.

On the Monday, Holmes and I took the train to Hastings. We made our way to Old Roar Waterfall on foot and set about constructing two hides in the heavy undergrowth. 2 p.m., the appointed time for our dénouement with Moran, came and went. We set off on the return journey to the bee-farm, eager to learn the outcome. Several police marksmen lay at ease, spread-eagled among the bushes. Lestrade was pacing up and down on Holmes's veranda, staring out across the Downs. It was clear from the Inspector's demeanour he was not relishing our return. Something had gone badly wrong.

We were a cricket pitch's length from the house when a shaken Lestrade turned and came hurrying towards us, ashen-faced. He stopped short, calling out, "It's no good your scowling, Mr. Holmes. We did our best. This time Moran was just too tricky for us."

With a heavy shudder he cried, "He was there, right in front of us, and then he wasn't. It was as though he possessed some supernatural power!"

Like the Cheshire Cat, our prey had appeared and disappeared, leaving nothing behind but a baleful snarl and an Italian revolver dropped in his hurry. It was to remain forever an unfathomable mystical experience in Lestrade's mind. Was the normally stolid Inspector right to believe he had come up against some supernatural power invested in Moran from his tiger-hunting days or – more likely – was it mere bungling? Had some sixth-sense warned the Colonel at the very last minute, even as he approached Holmes's hives? Or was one of Scotland Yard's marksmen now lolling on the grass an infiltrator, a surviving member of Professor Moriarty's old guard?

Bitterly disappointed, I turned to console my comrade. What the beleaguered Scotland Yard Inspector had taken to be a scowl was nothing of the sort. There *was* a strange gleam in Holmes's eye, but it was not one of disapproval. It was a gleam of intense satisfaction.

When Lestrade's men returned from their fruitless chase, they discovered a skep within a hundred yards of Holmes's farm. Five more were found in Friston Bottom, less than a mile away, containing enough Africanized killer bees to colonise and terrorise the whole of Sussex and nearby Kent. Contact with an eminent zoological society indicated the bees, native to the eastern and southern regions of Africa, might not survive even one chilly winter but to be certain the Army was called in. A flame-thrower platoon, replete with triple-layer mesh bee suits, rid England of the lethal creatures and after immediate compensation every hive of honey bees within two miles. To be entirely safe, Holmes embarked on the total replacement of his bee stock with *Apis mellifera ligustica*, a mild-mannered Italian subspecies of the western honeybee. Once the flamethrowers had done their work, the keen-eyed Tobias Gregson discovered a note attached to a nearby tree. It read, *'My dear Holmes and Watson, you must forgive my scribbled handwriting, but I am in somewhat of a hurry. You have foiled me this time, but I can assure you the matters between us still stand and indeed intensify. You may take it I shall be in touch. Yrs ever, SM.'*

There was a postscript: *'Niagara or Victoria Falls?'*

At a nearby Channel port, a man sporting a red and black silk cravat was reported boarding a Continental ferry in a great hurry.

Postscript

At Inspector Lestrade's request, the Suffolk Constabulary conducted a search of the farmhouse in the Stour Valley which Moran had been obliged to quit in such a hurry. They uncovered an exchange of letters between Moran and the British Beekeepers Association. Using a pseudonym, Moran claimed he wanted advice on cross-breeding bees to increase honey production. Were there any bees he should avoid? The answer came, '*You must at all costs avoid* A. m. scutellata, *the deadly hybrid of the Western honey bee, known as the* Tanganyikan *or* Killer Bee. *Do not allow even a single African killer bee queen into the hive. She hatches about two days before our British bee queens. She then proceeds to sting all the other queens to death, thus ensuring that her traits of aggressiveness are strengthened in her children.*'

It was the information he had needed to carry out his diabolical plot.

End

Die Weisse Frau

by Tim Symonds

It was 1916. I was home for a while from serving as a medical officer in Mesopotamia with my old regiment. I was at work at my surgery in London's Marylebone District. Through the window I glimpsed the charlady polishing the brass plate with 'Dr. John H. Watson M.D.' picked out in black. An overnight shower had washed away the grime from the maple-like leaves of the plane trees on Queen Anne Street, leaving them a lush green.

The Kaiser's War had been raging for two years. Almost within shouting distance of the South Coast millions of men faced each other across narrow stretches of no-man's-land. Each morning as the sun rose over the trenches the occasional stray dog caught up in the endless coils of barbed-wire jerked as it was hit by snipers adjusting their rifle sights for the day's human kill. A combination of entrenchments, machine gun nests, barbed wire, and artillery repeatedly inflicted severe casualties on the attackers and counter-attacking defenders. Gone were the days when battles lasted hardly a day, like Agincourt or the Battle of Hastings. Britain's expectation that the Boche would collapse before the first Christmas had long since faded into the illusion it had always been.

The war was having a powerful effect on the Home Front too. Almost every one of my patients arrived with a copy of William Le Queux's lurid tale *Spies of The Kaiser*, their hands trembling, convinced by *Spies* that a thousand trained German saboteurs were lying low in Britain, waiting for orders to strike. Le Queux encouraged patriotic Britons to follow his personal example: Go out at night, revolver in hand, searching for secret German signals, especially in the wooded countryside of Surrey.

By sunset, the last patient, the Rt. Hon. Sir _____ _____ had left. His role in His Majesty's Government gave him privileged knowledge of the state of the war. Barely able to hide his excitement, he told me to ready myself for some good news. A large-scale Allied offensive would soon be launched against the German Front Line astride a major river. The British Army would attack in huge numbers north of the river, the French to the south. He had one reservation: "Let's hope our Intelligence people have got this one right. Otherwise we could be in for a pasting."

A repeat of the Battle of Maiwand, I reflected ruefully, where in the long gone days of the Second Afghan War my Regiment fought Ayub Khan's tribesmen – and lost.

I was digesting the news when a sharp knocking at the tradesman's entrance heralded the arrival of a telegram.

"Dr. Watson, I presume?" queried the messenger-boy cockily. I handed him a generous sixpence and took the envelope and its contents back into electric light courtesy of the Hick Hargreaves reciprocating steam engines at Stowage. Telegrams were usually from my old comrade-in-arms Sherlock Holmes, issuing invitations to his isolated bee-farm on the Sussex Downs. To my surprise and equal pleasure, it was a message – though a mysterious one – from young Toby McCoy, the flat racing champion jockey. Only the previous year, he had won the two-thousand Guineas at Newmarket on *Pommerne*, on which I had placed a five-guinea bet at his urging. Would I find time to meet him with the greatest urgency, "*over certain matters of national importance*"? Rather than getting together at the Junior United Services Club, as we had on several occasions over the previous three or four years, could we rendezvous the following day at two o'clock near Hyde Park Corner, 'where the Rotten Row bridleway meets Park Lane'? McCoy planned to exercise the King's horses there and would saddle one up for me.

The telegram had a post-script: "*You should know we're selling off some fine cavalry horses deemed redundant in trench warfare.*"

I would direct this latter information to my landed-gentry patients. The likelihood of purchasing fine cavalry horses for my personal use was slim. With the increasing density of London's motorised traffic, the streets were fast becoming no-go areas for horses of any kind. Nevertheless, impressed by the sense of urgency thrumming through the telegram, I telephoned the nearby St. Mary's Hospital to arrange for a locum for the morrow.

The following day I lunched early and set off on foot. The walk through Hyde Park took me through a landscape of purple and gold from the carpet of crocuses and banks of daffodils scenting the damp air. 'Rotten Row' was a corruption of *Route du Roi*, the fashionable sandy stretch for carriages and horses made famous when the future King Edward VII triumphantly paraded the bewitching actress Lillie Langtry as his prize trophy.

McCoy was waiting with an impatient air. On catching sight of me, he trotted up with the second horse. With a glance around but hardly a word of greeting, he cantered off, remaining silent until the horses had broken a little sweat.

"Dr. Watson," he called across, "you must be wondering why all this secrecy!"

"I'm hoping it means you have a hot tip for the St. Leger Stakes," I said.

"It's rather more important than that," came a stern reply.

"More important than the St. Leger Stakes?" I exclaimed. "Surely only matters of war and peace could be more important!"

"As you say, Dr. Watson," McCoy responded. "It's very much a matter of war."

For the next ten minutes, the story he poured out intrigued and alarmed me in equal measure.

"Since we last met, Doctor, I have moved to an out-of-the-way part of England. My life has always been – and still is – solely concerned with horses. I pay little heed to public affairs – only what I read in the newspapers. Due to censorship, that's precious little."

"Whereabouts is this out-of-the-way place?" I asked.

"In Wiltshire. Near Marlborough. It's called Raffley Park."

"Raffley Park!" I exclaimed. "Isn't that the stud farm owned by a brewery magnate, Colonel Somebody-or-other, who believes breeding horses can be influenced by the sun and stars? I've heard he's so obsessed with horoscopes, he has astrological charts drawn up for all the foals he breeds...?"

"That was Colonel Walker, yes, but he's no longer the owner. Last year, under the greatest secrecy, the land and stables were purchased by the War Office, along with two stallions, broodmares, yearling fillies, and eight horses in training. It's become an Army Remount Depôt for transforming horses for war work. At first, we only handled the very finest officers' horses. That came to a halt once trench warfare started. Except in places like Palestine, cavalry charges have become a thing of the past. Mustangs and burros for hauling are what's most needed. They're pouring in from the American West. Raffley Park's job is to sort them out by waggon or pack units, and light, heavy, or siege artillery. You would know all about that from your time in the 5th Northumberland Fusiliers."

"Toby, the officers' horses. I should tell you right away it's most unlikely I am in the market for – "

"Nor would I expect you to be, Dr. Watson, living in Marylebone as you do," came the immediate return. "That would simply be your excuse to visit the Depôt."

My companion stared uneasily at other riders scattered among the well-spaced trees. He pointed towards the Serpentine.

29

"Let's take our horses over there, away from the others. I'm terrified we could be overheard."

I followed him in silence to the water's edge. I could see no reason why he should be calling on my services. I was a product of the British Army's medical training at Netley, not the Army Veterinary School at Aldershot, doctor to *Homo sapiens*, not *Equus ferus caballus*. As to being spied on in the middle of Hyde Park, it seemed absurd, yet his ruffled demeanour was palpable.

"Tell me," I began, when he interrupted with, "I hope, Doctor, I've convinced you of the importance of Raffley Park to the war effort?"

"Why, yes, I can see why it – "

Again he interrupted.

"Something happened last week. Something completely unexpected."

I waited.

"Completely unexpected," McCoy repeated. "During the night, two German airships flew over us. Really low. One of them was the Zeppelin L-13. Their firebombs got direct hits on the stables. The wood and straw were ablaze in seconds. More than half the horses were suffocated by the smoke or burnt and had to be put down. The rest will need months of rehabilitation. The Army says to lose a horse is worse than losing a man. Men are replaceable. Right now, horses aren't."

"A terrible thing to happen," I remarked, "but this is a nasty war. The air above us is only the latest theatre. Surely that sort of thing is to be expected…?"

"Nasty it is," he agreed, "but there was something odd about this attack. Maybe it was chance, but it was the way the Zeppelins came in to drop their bombs."

"Go on," I urged. The old warhorse in me was starting to snort and paw.

"I shouldn't tell you this, but the Royal Garrison Artillery have got two motorised sections in the fields near us. It's their responsibility to defend us. They shift their positions every week or so. It happened that neither of the units was sited along the route the airships came in at us. It's as though the enemy knew exactly which approach was safe that particular night – and worse, exactly the night it would pay off to come and drop firebombs on us. A fresh batch of five-hundred horses arrived only hours before. Between you and me, I've been wondering how the Boche knew. A day earlier and there'd have been no horses. One day later and most of the horses would have been dispersed to other Remount depôts in Kent. We'd have been left with less than one hundred."

"My dear fellow," I exclaimed, "we've long since rounded up all Germany's spies in Liverpool or Southampton or whichever ports these horses come to. It could be completely by chance that the Zeppelins came on that particular route – wind direction perhaps – and on that particular night."

"You may be right, Doctor," McCoy replied. "Nevertheless...if it's not likely there are any spies left at the ports, could there be someone right among us – on the staff of Raffley Park?"

I leaned forward and clapped him on the shoulder.

"Toby, look. If you really feel there's a serious possibility one of the staff is an enemy spy, then I'd be happy to come down for a night or two. I'll entice my old comrade Sherlock Holmes to come, too. As you suggest, we could come incognito, pretending we're looking at chargers for sale."

"Dr. Watson, I would welcome that very much!" McCoy exclaimed joyfully. "There's one more matter you need to know. Except for a couple of us men riders helping out, it's the only Remount depôt in England run entirely by the feminine sex, mostly from the gentlewoman class, the sort who rode to hounds before the war. The latest arrival went to finishing school on the Continent. Even the boss is a woman – Lady Mabel, an American. She's married to Major-General ------- at the War Office."

I dismounted and passed the horse's reins to him with, "I'll await your invitation, Toby. Meantime, tell me, what's the word on the St. Leger Stakes this September?"

"A chestnut trained by Fred Darling. You'd do well to keep an eye on him."

"By the name of?"

"*Hurry On.*"

"Worth a five guinea bet?" I asked.

"Every penny. I'll be back in touch if anything else occurs at the Depôt." At which the champion jockey turned away and rode off in the direction of Buckingham Palace.

Weeks passed. The unusual encounter with Toby McCoy drifted from my memory. We had not set a definite date for a visit to Raffley Park, though I solicited and received Sherlock Holmes's assent in principal. Then in high summer, a letter marked '*Personal*' arrived, postmarked Swindon.

Dear Dr. Watson (McCoy wrote),

It won't be reported in the newspapers, but Zeppelin L-13 and friend were back last night. Again it was just hours after we'd fetched a large batch of horses from _____ Docks. Lots of damage and a hundred horses lost (though luckily none of us bipeds). The Royal Garrison Artillery had just moved their pom-poms to cover the first approach, but this time the Zepps came from a completely different direction. Something serious is going on. Either there really is a spy in the city of Newport News, where the horses board ship that side of the Atlantic, or in _____, or there's someone much closer to home. We're in line for a further batch of horses. Everyone's extremely jittery. Can you come down soonest, and bring Mr. Sherlock Holmes with you? He should be dressed in Mufti. Otherwise people here will catch on in an instant.

32

The journey by train took Holmes and me through a Wiltshire landscape hardly changed in four-thousand years. We passed impressive signs of human activity far back into the Stone Age – barrows and ancient hill forts and great sarsen stones, the post-glacial remains of a cap of Cenozoic silcrete that once covered much of southern England – a dense, hard rock created from sand bound by a silica cement.

Holmes had chosen one of his favourite disguises, a Free Church clergyman in a broad black hat, baggy trousers and white tie, with the general look of peering and benevolent curiosity I described in the case of 'A Scandal in Bohemia'. He could have chosen to impersonate the more abundant ministers of the Church of England, except it was a criminal offence. Impersonating a minister of any cult different from that of the official religion of the State was not.

Toby McCoy was waiting for us at the railway station. We shook hands. He was seated arms akimbo on a smart new motor-cycle. "A Premier," he told us, "supplied by the Army." I noticed his long black curls had been shorn like the sheep on nearby Salisbury Plains.

McCoy stared at my comrade for several seconds. Finally, he asked, "Is it truly him? Mr. Sherlock Holmes?"

Although the Italians say *"l'abito non fa il monaco"* – the cassock doesn't make the clergyman – the truth is, for the majority of people the visual impact of clerical garb *does* make the clergyman.

"It's he," I replied. "We can simply address him as 'Parson' when anyone's about."

With a wide grin McCoy pointed at his own hair. "I thought I was a civilian but then out of the blue I received a telegram last week telling me to turn up at the War Office. They said, "We'll commission you as a Second Lieutenant in the Intelligence Corps". I even got £50 to buy my uniform and equipment, along with some instruction on how to salute and who to salute."

Recalling my own first military kitting-out at Gieves in Saville Row, I asked, "Where did you go to buy your uniform?"

"Moss Brothers. Covent Garden. Thirty shillings second-hand. I'll mostly wear it when I go to meet the horses at the Docks."

Lodgings had been arranged for us at a public house going by the odd name of *Who'd A Thought It*, a convenient quarter-of-a-mile or so from the Remount depôt gates. Speaking quietly, McCoy related how Lady Mabel had given him permission for our visit and revealed the next batch of horses would be unloaded at the port in a few days' time.

We deliberately spent a further few minutes at the station exit talking about trivial matters. McCoy laughed inordinately when any of us made anything resembling a joke, yet behind the humorous blarney I discerned the same shadow – not exactly of fear, but an anxiety as when runners line up for the starting gun at the start of a horse-race.

"As usual, the mounts will stay here just for the one night," he informed us. "About three hundred and fifty horses will travel onwards the next day to Remount depôts at Romsey and Ormskirk, or Swaythling."

Our young friend said he had extracted a firm promise from Lady Mabel not to mention the arrival date of the next batch of horses to anyone whatsoever. He was quite certain he and she were the only two people in Raffley Park and nearby villages who knew the exact morning the ship would dock. He hoped we could stay until the new remounts arrived at Raffley Park, "though, gentlemen," he added thoughtfully, "in light of the last Zeppelin attack, I shall understand if you prefer to take your leave a day or two before, just in case. One hit with a firebomb and the pub'll go up just like the stables, even worse."

Luggage in hand, we set off. As we approached our lodgings, McCoy said, "I could meet you here this evening. I'll just say you're old friends from the race-course though . . ." He looked dubiously at Holmes's clergyman's dress, "...your appearance, sir, may inhibit the drinking. If I'm lucky," he added, "the new girl – the one I mentioned – her name's Adrienne, might be there."

A slight flush came to his cheeks. "She's taken to coming to the pub along with four or five of the other girls. They've formed a sort of knitting circle. Scarves and socks for the occupied Belgians. They're always pulling old bits of wool clothing apart to knit into small squares which get sewn together into blankets."

McCoy turned to leave. "I'm quite taken with Adrienne," he added unnecessarily, "though we haven't yet exchanged a word ...I'll say *au revoir*, Parson and Mister...er..."

"Wilson will do," I said.

Holmes said, "Hold on a moment, Toby. I want you to do something important. The horses will arrive soon, you say?"

McCoy nodded.

"Which exact day?" Holmes pursued.

"Friday evening."

"And you say this fact is known to no-one here except Lady Mabel and yourself?"

"Not another living soul. Even Lady Mabel never knows until a few days ahead. Anyway, this time we've told everyone the next lot are going straight to Romney Marsh, over in Kent."

"Then I want you to do something," Holmes continued, "one person at a time, as though in the greatest confidence. Let out that the next consignment is due this Friday, here at Raffley Park, not Romney Marsh. Do this also at the '*Who'd A Thought If*'. Just say everyone thinks the horses are going to Kent, but give a knowing look and inform them that's not true. Do so as soon as possible. If there's a spy around, they'll need enough time to pass the information to the enemy."

McCoy and I stared incredulously at Holmes.

"But they *are* coming here," McCoy said.

"Precisely. Make it look like a couple of drinks have loosened the tongue. Immediately look embarrassed and swear them to silence. Have you got that all right?"

"If that's want you want, I'll do as you say...Parson," came the perplexed reply.

We watched as the small figure set off across the fields.

"Parson," I said quietly, "I was as surprised as our young friend when you told him to blurt out details of the horses' arrival. Surely it'd be safer to pretend they're going to Romney..."

"It's a risk, yes," my comrade interrupted. "But it's a risk we have to take. If there's a spy at the Raffley Park depôt, we must catch whoever it is *in flagrante*."

In the morning we ate a light breakfast at the pub before setting off for the depôt to meet Toby. He signed us in at the sentry-box and led the way towards a set of isolated stables holding the officers' horses for sale. As soon as he was certain there was no-one else around, McCoy stopped in his tracks. His look became serious.

"Something happened last night, after you went off to bed," he began. "Something I think you should hear before we meet tonight at the *Who'd A Thought It*. I don't know how to explain it."

"Go on," said Holmes.

In a low tone, the jockey related how the knitting circle had been in the pub's bar for more than an hour. "First the other girls left. Adrienne - you remember I mentioned her - followed, but a good ten minutes later. Before leaving, she turned and waved goodbye to me."

A short while later Toby realised she had left her knitting behind.

"I knew it was hers because I noticed the others were knitting wool squares, but Adrienne was, as usual, working on one of her scarves. This one was mostly grey with bits of different colours."

He blushed. "I saw it as a heaven-sent excuse to break the ice. I picked up the knitting and ran out after her. She'd only gone about fifty yards. I must have given her a shock – after all, it was dark. The moon's just the one night over the quarter. She certainly gave quite a start when I called out her name. I suppose after recent events, everyone's nerves are a bit raw. She seemed extremely relieved when I explained why I'd come haring after her."

"And then?" Holmes asked.

"I handed her the scarf, and so as not to make her uncomfortable I told her I was returning to the pub. I started back, but I remembered there've been sightings of a rabid fox hereabouts. The quickest way to the depot is over some open fields. The fox could easily be there. Or someone might...one of the lads of the village with a few pints in him might...might try it on, nothing harmful, you know, but it could upset her ..."

"So you offered to accompany her?" I asked. "Well, why not!"

"Not exactly accompany her, no, Doctor. I decided I would keep her in sight while she wended her way, so that if anything untoward took place – "

I ended his sentence for him: " – you could come to the rescue of a damsel in distress!"

He explained that Adrienne had started off in a direct line towards the depot, but "Quite soon something odd occurred. She stepped off the main path and made her way to the copse, the one with the tall pines with blue-green leaves and orange-red bark."

I had noticed the small wood earlier.

"*Pinus sylvestris*," I said. "Scots Pine."

"If you say so, Doctor," came the answer. "Anyway, she gave a good look round before she entered the copse. I couldn't think why she would go in there. There's just a ruddy great hole in the centre where the Royal Garrison Artillery put one of their Anti-Aircraft guns, a QF 1-pounder pom-pom, but it soon turned out they couldn't shoot at anything coming at them from the sky until it was right overhead. Because of the tall trees, you see," he added superfluously. "So they took it away."

"Do continue," I encouraged him.

"I stayed my distance but kept my eye on the place where Adrienne should come out of the trees to carry on towards the depôt. She didn't come out for more than half-an-hour. I was freezing cold when she did at last appear. From there, it was easy to see her in the starlight and be certain she was all right, so I followed along behind her, ducking now and then into the long grass whenever she looked back, until she reached home."

"And she entered through the main gate?" Holmes asked, looking intently at the jockey.

"Funny you ask that, Mr. Holmes," came the reply. "No, she didn't. She got through a hole in the fence. I never knew there was a gap there. I suppose by then she realised it was getting late and going through the fence was quicker, or maybe she'd forgotten her pass to show the sentry."

There was a moment's silence. Holmes asked, "You told 'Mr. Wilson' here that Adrienne went to finishing school on the Continent. Do you know where?"

"It was in Switzerland."

"Which part?"

"She mentioned it once. The name stuck in my mind. Zugerberg. I remember overhearing her saying most of the girls from her English boarding school went to Château Mont-Choisi – that's where they speak French – but Adrienne went to school in the German-speaking part, high up in the mountains. Ah!" he exclaimed, pointing at a line of stables just ahead, "here we are. These were the only stables left undamaged by the Zeppelins. It's where we keep the officers' chargers, the ones for sale. As I said, with mostly trench warfare, chargers like these aren't much in demand any longer."

I heard Holmes ask, "A last question, Toby. You said 'one of her scarves'. Presumably you've noticed Adrienne knitting them before?"

"Yes," came the answer. "Twice. Seems most of England's women are knitting away at things for the poor old Belgians."

Before sunset, Holmes and I said goodbye to our jockey friend. On the way, we diverted from the path and crept like poachers into the copse. The thick layer of pine needles muffled our footsteps. The greens, browns and blacks of Holmes's clergyman's outfit provided excellent camouflage among the trees. The Scots Pine gave way to a scattering of Majesty Oaks, almost certainly propagated by the activity of jays. We went deeper until we came to a glade perhaps twenty-feet square. A battered tin sheep trough lay to one side, as though cleared from the centre.

I peered around. "There's nothing here, Holmes," I said. "Not even the large dug-out Toby said the Anti-Aircraft artillery stood in. Either we're in the wrong clearing, or someone's filled it in. We're wasting our time."

Holmes pointed at a tall oak. "That tree, Watson, the one with the thick ivy growing up it."

"What of it?"

"Go and tug some of the vines from the trunk, if you don't mind."

I did so until I exposed the smooth, silvery brown bark of the lower trunk.

"My heavens!" I exclaimed. My tugging had exposed a wire tucked among the ivy's shiny dark evergreen leaves. "A Marconi antenna, Holmes. Wireless telegraphy. Of course! The Royal Garrison Artillery chaps must have left it behind."

"If you say so," Holmes rejoined. "And if I'm not mistaken . . ." he added, stepping further into the small clearing, "we'll find something else of interest under the soil here. Ah! In fact...come here, Watson. Take a look at this."

He was standing by a round metal pipe jutting up through the leafy ground cover. "A drain pipe?" I spluttered. "Why would..."

"A drain pipe, certainly, Watson, but not for conducting water. It's a breathing hole. I repeat, if I'm not badly mistaken, there's something of considerable interest beneath our feet. Look for a square outline, something about the size of a cucumber frame."

"There!" I exclaimed, pointing.

Even as I spoke, Holmes was striding to the nearest patch of undergrowth. He reached into it and yanked at something. At the spot I had indicated, a lid about three feet square sprang open. The hideout was so well concealed that no-one walking over the roofing would notice the ground beneath his feet remained hollowed out.

"It's getting dark. We must hurry," Holmes ordered. "Keep an eye open for anything spies might use."

Swiftly we descended a small ladder. "What sort of spy things are we to look for?" I enquired.

"Codes. Secret inks," came the whispered reply. "Any sort of night-signalling apparatus to guide the Zeppelins, glass delay-action incendiaries disguised as carpenters' pencils."

My foot contacted a Tilley lamp. I lit it, and we found ourselves in a space roughly six feet deep, the floor about ten feet by ten feet.

"Adrienne's emergency exit," Holmes murmured, pointing to a short flight of steps cut into the earth at the far corner. "She takes no risks. That's what the abandoned sheep trough is hiding."

Four little blue flowers, dried violets, had been carefully placed in a niche next to a candle. Attached to the wall was a map showing the region's ancient archaeology, Avebury Circle and Stonehenge particularly recognisable. Further along the wall was a small metal box on a make-shift shelf.

"Holmes, no matter what reason she has for visiting this bunker, Adrienne can't be a spy," I assured him. "This is a Marconi wireless apparatus set up only as a receiver. At best, she could receive messages from Berlin, but she can't send any to them. Surely this lets her off the hook."

"I'm afraid it proves nothing, Watson," came the terse reply. "There are good reasons for spies not to use transmitters. The principal one is noise. A receiver alone, powered by a battery, would scarcely be heard, even if someone is standing above us in the clearing. She'd need at least a four-horse-power motor for a transmitter. That size of generator would be heard for half-a-mile, especially at night. It would easily be heard by anyone on the footpath we take to the *Who'd A Thought It*. The best and most effective way to lessen the sound is to run the generator's exhaust pipe through water, but that would require a much larger water-tank than that sheep-trough.

"Even then, the water would discolour quickly and draw the attention of an unexpected visitor. Also, the smell of the exhaust going up that pipe would carry a long way in a breeze. The reason for using the radio only as a receiver allows Berlin to confirm the Zeppelins are coming. This gives their spy sufficient time to come to the safety of this bunker while the fire-bombing's going on. That is what she must have done during the Zeppelin attacks on Raffley Park. I wager you excellent odds that she has to rendezvous with Berlin at a precise time to receive her instructions, which explains why she held back until the other girls left the pub."

I stared at Holmes, baffled.

"I take your point about *receiving* information," I said, "but if Adrienne really is a spy, as you seem set on proving, how is she telling the Boche when to send over their Zeppelins in the first place, and from which direction they should approach to avoid the British guns?"

"Watson, my dear fellow," Holmes replied with a now-familiar look in his eye – the look of a man on a hunt – "that's exactly what we need to discover. And quickly too. We can start by searching this bunker with the utmost care."

After a few intensive minutes we gave up. Holmes muttered, "Nothing except those four dried violets. It's clear she doesn't have a way to transmit messages over the air. She must have some other way to contact Berlin. The question is, how?"

He pointed at the Tilley lamp. "Be a good fellow and extinguish that light. I think it's time we went back to the pub. Go out ahead of me. I'll close the lid. We'll scatter a few leaves over the entrance to cover our tracks."

As I clambered up the ladder, Holmes called after me, "Keep all this quiet, even from your friend Toby McCoy. Without an overt act or a confession, we are left only with circumstantial evidence, certainly not sufficient proof of manifest treason. Without the one or the other, we can't bring a charge against anyone for the capital crime of consorting with the enemy."

Evening had set in by the time we arrived at the *Who'd A Thought It*. As we entered the Lounge Bar, Toby McCoy beckoned from the far corner. On our way we crossed the picturesque old room with sanded floors and high-backed settees, passing the lively group of young women who made up the knitting circle. The girls raised their knitting needles in a friendly hallo, giving a collective giggle at the sight of a cleric among them.

Piled-up plates of freshly-baked bread and large chunks of cheese arrived. We ate in silence, Holmes and I pondering the afternoon's events. Toby McCoy, too, was silent.

At the end of the meal, my comrade suddenly said, "Wilson, you and Toby have always wanted to know a bit about knitting, haven't you! Why don't you wander over to those spare chairs next to Miss Adrienne at the knitting table."

"On the contrary, my dear Holmes," I replied, forgetting for the moment to address him as "Parson", "I assure you I haven't the faintest interest in learning knitting!"

"Oh yes, you have," Holmes said firmly. He gestured at McCoy. "As does Toby here."

Holmes grabbed my arm. His voice dropped to a whisper. "Merely a device, Watson, to occasion another meeting between her and our love-smitten friend. While you're talking, get a good look at the objects the girls are knitting, including Adrienne's scarf. Looks like she's nearly finished it. Ask her to let you try a stitch or two."

In the morning we set off for the railway station. The stationmaster put down *The Marlborough Morning News* when we entered his office. He beckoned us to take a seat.

"May I help you, Parson?" he said to Holmes, with a separate friendly nod to me.

"I believe you may, Stationmaster," my comrade began. "We've heard many of the church congregations in territories conquered by the Germans are in terrible straits because of the shortages of clothing. My parishioners over in Ashby St. Mary want to knit items for the Belgians – that is my *women* parishioners, of course!" he added with a chortle. "If we send parcels, how would they go to Belgium? By what route?"

"Let's see," the stationmaster replied, putting on a thinking expression, "I don't know about Ashby St. Mary, but I can tell you the route from here. A young woman from Raffley Park has taken to sending parcels for the Belgians. One was put on the train only this morning. They best go via London to Folkestone. That's because Folkestone is the best port for Flushing. Flushing's in Holland," he added for our

43

enlightenment, "and the trains have to go through Holland to get to Belgium, you see."

"I presume it takes quite some time for a parcel to get to Belgium, then?" Holmes pursued.

"No, Parson," came the reply. "That's the surprising thing. It doesn't. The trains run just as quick as they did before the War. In fact quicker. Less traffic on the rails, except for when they're moving troops around. Say you post a parcel from here in the morning. It'll go on the next fast train to London, sorted, then an hour or so later sent down to the coast, pass through customs, on to a cross-Channel ferry to Holland, and on the next train from Flushing to the Belgian frontier. Bob's your uncle! Hardly more than twenty-four hours I'd say, and your parcel will reach its destination."

We thanked the stationmaster and closed his office door behind us. "Folkestone it is, Watson," Holmes said in a low voice, "and as fleet as we've ever been. We'll take a cab and board an express train at Swindon. I've got my ordinary clothes under this attire. If we leave now, with luck we'll be back before anyone notes our absence."

"What do you expect to find in Folkestone?" I asked. "If it's you-know-who you're concerned with, assuming you aren't completely wrong, surely she wouldn't risk putting anything in a parcel going through customs."

"I've no doubt you're right, Watson, she wouldn't," came the reply. "Except her knitting."

The enigmatic response was followed by, "If I'm wrong, Watson, then England is in serious trouble. We can expect the worst. The fire-bombings are likely to continue. Without a good supply of horses to haul the heavy loads our guns won't move an inch, vital *matériel* to our armies will cease ..."

His words trailed away.

It was no good pressing my comrade. He had the most irritating habit of playing the stage conjuror, pulling a rabbit out of the hat at the time which suited him and not a moment earlier.

We changed stations in London. In a remarkably short time we disembarked at Folkestone. A porter pointed out the Customs House.

Even in a provincial port Holmes, no longer in disguise, was recognised immediately as England's most famous investigating detective. Assistance was instant, confidentiality assured. A rapid search was conducted for a parcel for Belgium with an address written in a woman's hand. Within minutes we were in possession.

"Look at the unusual knots, Watson," my comrade remarked, carefully unpicking the string. "One overhand knot embracing another."

Amused, I asked, 'Why would that come to your attention, Holmes?" I asked.

"I believe it's known as the True Lover's Knot," he replied.

The parcel fell open. Out came a dozen or so square woollen patches, followed by a long grey scarf with a few splashes of bright colours.

I picked up the sturdy wrapping paper and shook it.

"Look, Holmes. You can see it contains only the scarf and the squares. There's nothing else in the package. Thank Heavens!" I exclaimed, deeply relieved for young McCoy's sake. "If there's a spy at Raffley Park, it can't be Adrienne."

My comrade pushed the woollen squares to the side and spread the scarf out on the customs bench. He tugged out a ten-power silver-and-chrome magnifying glass from a voluminous pocket of his Poshteen Long Coat.

"It's the same scarf all right," I assured him, "the one she was knitting at the *Who'd A Thought It*. I recognise the design."

"What in particular do you remember?" Holmes asked. I pointed to one end. "Those five vertical lines in that sort of cartouche. She was working on them when Toby and I sat with her, pretending we wanted to learn how to knit."

He threw me a quizzical look. "And what do you make of them?" he asked.

"I make nothing of them, Holmes," I retorted. "They're just part of the pattern. What else could they be?"

"And that circle of 'bumps'?" Holmes continued, pointing. I shook my head.

"Again, what am I supposed to make of them? Adrienne said something about 'stocking stitches'. I even assumed she was making long stockings – not scarves."

"You might bear in mind, Watson, that some of the best spies in this war are not our agents in occupied territories, with their cloaks and daggers and bits of rice paper squeezed into bicycle valves. The hardest to spot are simple housewives knitting innocent-looking patterns."

"You mean like Madame Defarge, the *tricoteuse* in *A Tale Of Two Cities?*" I scoffed. "Really, Holmes! That was something Charles Dickens just dreamed up! Adrienne openly says she's doing this knitting to send to the Belgians. Surely she'd keep that quiet if she really was a spy."

"It should become a dictum of yours, Watson, that false stories containing elements of truth have the longest legs. Let's start with the five lines of stitches," he went on. "What day of the week do we expect the next consignment of horses?"

"Friday," I returned, lowering my voice. "If you mean each line of stitching represents one day of the week, starting on a Monday, then (I began to count of my fingers) Monday to Tuesday, one day. Tuesday to Wednesday, two days. Wednesday to Thursday, three days. Thursday to Friday...that's only four days. Five lines would mean this Saturday. If it's a code, she's given them the wrong day, a day too late. Most of the horses will have been moved on."

"But what if I tell you Germans count the days of the week from the Sunday, not Monday?" my comrade replied.

A cold hand clutched at my heart.

"These lines of stitches," he continued. "Knit one, purl one – alternate rows of plain and purl stitches. That's what's known as 'stocking stitches'. She wasn't about to knit stockings. Remember the archaeological map on the wall of the bunker? She was knitting features in the landscape. Barrows and sarsen stones would easily be visible from more than a thousand feet up, even on a cloudy night. That's how she tells the Zeppelins the safest approach. Look, here's Stonehenge on Salisbury Plain outlined in blue stitching. And there's the outcrop of sarsen stones in the Savernake Forest. And this," he pointed at an oblong burst of stitching, "is the ancient barrow just to the north of Raffley Park. Here we come to the Marlborough Downs – and a second set of Sarsen Stones. All outlined in blue."

My spirits sank. I was beginning to reach the inevitable conclusion. "So what are those red lines?" I asked.

"That one's the old Roman road, and that . . ." Holmes said, tracing his hand along the knitting, "...the Ridgeway."

I pointed at a dotted line I didn't recall from the archaeological map. "And this green wiggle?" I asked.

"That's the route the Zeppelins are to follow. The scarf is as clear as a Royal Automobile Club route-map. The spy will have scouted the area on a bicycle to be sure there are no anti-aircraft emplacements along it. There's no doubt about it, Watson. That's the direction the Hun's airships will come from this time."

He replaced the scarf in its packing and carefully retied the string using the same neat symmetrical knots. "Holmes," I gasped. "Surely we aren't going to – "

"Let her route map go on its way? Of course we are, Watson. Our little ruse worked. Toby succeeded in letting the secret out, just as I planned. But not one word to him about all this. His infatuation with her might cause him to go astray and warn her.'

Friday arrived. Just after sunset, Holmes and I re-entered the dug-out. Inside we stayed completely silent. My heart pounded. I was about to break the long silence with a question when his hand shot up.

"Silence, Watson," he hissed. "I hear a rustle."

Sure enough, a moment later the trapdoor swung up. Someone came to the opening and descended. The breathing was fast, as though the approach had been made in a great hurry. The figure bent down and put a flame to the Tilley Lamp.

Then Adrienne turned and saw us. She stared at the Army service revolver in my hand.

"So," she said, "you've found my hideout. I like to come here to – "

Holmes interrupted. "Before you give us some absurd reason for being here, you should know we went to Folkestone and caught up with your latest package." He pointed at the archaeological map on the wall. "It was very clever the way you placed the purl and knit stitches on the scarf to show the sarsen stones and barrows the Zeppelins should pick out. Each time you gave the enemy an exact route to approach Raffley Park which would by-pass our guns."

She stood motionless looking at us. After a long silence she said, "Where is the scarf now?"

"We sent the parcel on to the address you gave," I replied. "It turns out it's a shop-front for Chef 111b, the German Military service, not a harmless group of Belgian citizens. Now that the horses are here, we expect the Zeppelins at any moment. You are a traitor to your country, Adrienne. In war, the penalty for such betrayal is death by firing squad or the hangman's noose."

"You don't understand, Mr. Wilson," she whispered, tears rising in her eyes. "I had good reason for this so-called betrayal."

"Then the parson here and I should like to hear it," came my severe response.

Her story tumbled out. Her family had been well-to-do but restrictive. A year before the War broke out, she was sent to traditional finishing school near Zurich. It focused on teaching social graces as a preparation for entry into upper class society. "My father," she explained, showing remarkable erudition for a woman so young, "was *laudator temporis acti* – a 'praiser of time past'."

Her language tutor at the finishing school was a handsome young man by the name of Ulrich Hoffmeyer from Göttingen, a university town deep in the countryside of Lower Saxony.

"Uli was brought from Germany because the school wanted us to learn a good accent," she explained, "not *Schwiizerdütsch*, the dialect they speak around Zurich." Uli waited for her every day after her classes. "That spring, we walked away from the whole world and sat among the drifts of tiny crocuses and gentians and primroses." After some months Hoffmeyer asked her to marry him, "and I accepted immediately."

She failed to inform her parents because of their prejudiced views against all Germans. After her return, Uli and she corresponded furtively, even more so after the war broke out. "Uli wrote to say he was returning to Germany. Then the letters ceased."

She feared he had been sent to the Front Line, even that he may have died at the Battle of the Marne. "Then six months ago, something happened," she continued. "A letter arrived. It made me jump for joy. It was sent from Sweden, but it was from Uli. I recognised his handwriting at once." The letter was in a code he used when he wrote to her at her parents' farm. "Somehow, he heard I was working at my first Army Remount depôt, up North. He was safe in Berlin, in the Imperial German Army, the *Deutsches Heer*, working for the Chief of the German General Staff, General Erich von Falkenhayn."

By now the words were tumbling out. "There was something special he wanted to ask me. It could make a difference to whether we would ever see each other again. He said there were a considerable number of people in the General Staff who felt things were not turning out as they expected. The French had rallied at Verdun and halted the German Army's advance on Paris. The British were not being driven back into the Channel. There were already signs of a stalemate. Uli and others in the German General Staff believed it might be possible to get von Falkenhayn to suggest a cessation of hostilities between England and Germany. But he said there was a serious problem: The Kaiser! Wilhelm's pride was 'too much on the line' to accept an armistice."

She hurried on. "Uli said that millions of ordinary Germans didn't want to go on fighting England. In German, 'England' means 'the Land of the Angels'. It had been a terrible slip-up."

"I presume your fiancé came up with a solution?" I heard Holmes ask, the words not altogether lacking a sarcastic undertone.

She nodded. "He said in trench warfare, all information collected on the battle front only gave a local and more-or-less temporary advantage over the opponent. They needed to know more. Uli said if they could break the stale-mate on the battlefields, the Kaiser might agree to a ceasefire and discuss peace. He said that awful as it must seem, if the German air force could make a couple of spectacular strikes and cripple England's ability to wage war in Flanders through the lack of horses, the heavy ones in particular, the Kaiser's *Selbstachtung* – his *amour propre* – would be satisfied. He might agree to discussing terms for peace."

My revolver felt heavy in my hand. "And that's when you first informed him through your knitting code when the horses were about to arrive?" I pursued.

Again, now almost indiscernibly, she uttered the word, "Yes".

"And for fear your treachery might be discovered if you stayed on too long at your first depôt, Chef 111b ordered you to ask to be moved to another Remount depôt," Holmes broke in, "which is why you took up employment here at Raffley Park."

Again she nodded.

Unable to hide my despair, I asked, "Adrienne, couldn't you see this Ulrich Hoffmeyer was taking advantage of your puppy love? The Kaiser's *amour propre* be damned! I doubt if the *Deutsches Heer* has any intention of calling for a ceasefire. Obtaining such information on our military resources could help to create a decisive advantage for the Hun, not some sort of balance! Without horses to draw our vehicles in the mud of Flanders, our Army would soon be starved of food and clothing and ammunition. The troops would be overwhelmed in no time. If we hadn't caught you, you could have gone on to one Remount depôt after another. Within a year, the Boche could be marching down Whitehall."

"I want this war to end," she wailed, tears welling up in her eyes. "I want to get back with Uli."

I expected Holmes to remark it was much too late for that, that the gallows would intervene, when to my astonishment he said, "That might be possible one day, but there would be a condition. Shall we say a necessary correction to the balance of treason?"

The words sounded the more incongruous coming from a man attired in a Free Church clergyman's dress.

"At the previous Remount depôt," Holmes continued, "you passed information to the enemy which had damaging consequences. You left there and came to Raffley Park and repeated the same treason. By sheer luck, none of the staff died. It's only fair if now you find a way to pass an equal amount of military information back to your own country."

The young woman fell quiet, looking from Holmes's face to mine and back. The words "Do I have a choice?" fell from her lips.

"Certainly," Holmes said in an accommodating tone. "Cooperate with us and live, or, as you see, my friend has an old Army service revolver from his India days."

Holmes continued, "You hesitate. Let me spell it out. You can cooperate, or you can walk over to that wall right now and my friend will shoot you through the forehead. I assure you he will pull the trigger. This bunker will become your tomb."

"I suggest you cooperate, Adrienne," I begged, hoping fervently she would take up Holmes's unexpected offer.

Seconds ticked by. At last her defiant look gave way to one of near despair.

Holmes spoke. "I take it from your look you accept our terms. You speak excellent German. You have already been trained in wireless telegraphy. We shall expect you to balance your crime against England by fleeing immediately to Occupied Europe and sending back military information – the state of airfields, location of ammunition depots, and above all, railway intelligence – troop movements and so on. Go to your quarters and collect your things. Return here straight afterwards. Speak to no-one. Make use of the hole in the fence already known to you. At the earliest hour, we shall escort you to General Headquarters in London. You must sign the 1911 Official Secrets Act. You'll then join the Secret Service section of MI6."

Holmes pointed at the wireless receiver. "In turn, we shall make sure this bunker is completely cleared. No-one here will ever know you spied for the Germans. I suggest you leave behind a note addressed to Lady Mabel. Explain your nerves have been badly shattered. You want to get away from danger for a while, somewhere so remote it will seem the War is a million miles away."

"And what do I tell the Germans?" she asked, her voice quavering.

"That you heard an MI5 investigation into the fire-bombings was imminent. You feared someone would put two and two together because your previous depôt was also firebombed by airships. It might be a matter of days, hours even, and you would be found out, so you had to flee."

He added, "Go now. If you do not return here within the half-hour, I can assure you neither my friend Mr. Wilson here nor I can save you. A watch will be put in place at every port and airfield. Within a matter of days, you will be captured, summarily tried, and put before a firing-squad and buried in an unmarked grave. Your family will be told the reason why. They will live with the shame of living out their lives knowing their daughter was a traitor to her country."

I intervened. "Assuming you agree to these terms, the Germans may ask the identity of the person MI5 planned to call in to uncover the traitor."

I waved the pistol at my companion.

"In which case you may reveal the identity of the person standing before you."

"And your name, Parson?" she asked, staring doubtfully at the clerical outfit.

"Sherlock Holmes," came the answer.

Without the blink of an eyelid she turned to me and asked coolly, "So do I assume you are not Mr. Wilson, but the famous Dr. Watson?"

I bowed. "If not as famous as you make me sound, I am certainly Dr. Watson."

For some reason I cannot explain, I felt a surge of warmth towards this young woman fighting to keep her composure. "Will you be able to get through the borders and check-points?" I asked more gently.

"Yes," she replied. "I have a code name that can be checked. It will get me through."

"And this *nom-de-guerre?*" Holmes asked.

"*Die Weisse Frau*," came the reply. "'*The White Lady*'." She pointed upwards. "But what of the Zeppelins? They'll be coming over at any moment."

"We've taken care of that," I heard Holmes reply.

I pointed across to the four dried little violets. "The flowers. Are they some sort of cipher?"

"In a way, yes," she replied. Tears sprang to her eyes. "Those violets were the last thing Uli gave me when I left Switzerland. He picked them for me on the slopes of the Swiss mountain. One for each of the kisses he gave me. First on the forehead, then on either cheek, and last of all a kiss on the mouth."

At that very moment the rat-tat-tat of half a dozen Royal Garrison Artillery pom-poms broke out, barely muffled by the layer of leaves and branches above our heads. The thud of the shells was interspersed with the crack of Pomeroy 0.303in. calibre explosive bullets. The firing continued for several minutes and all fell silent. Holmes gestured at the open trapdoor.

"It's time you were on your way," he told our captive.

The next morning brought an unexpected bonus. Among the twisted wreckage of the two airships, a valuable and recently-introduced German signal book was recovered intact.

Before sun-up, Holmes and I took Adrienne to the railway station for the journey to London. It had been a long night spent agonising over her fate. Sleep had eluded me, even when Holmes took over the watch. Whenever I looked across at our young captive, she was leaning on her suitcase, staring down at the dried violets in her hand. It seemed clear to me Holmes was sending her to certain death. The Zeppelins had come in once again on her knitted instructions but this time they had run into a very heavy barrage and been utterly destroyed. The crew's bodies had been burnt to cinders before they struck the Wiltshire soil.

The St. Leger Stakes took place in the September. My five guineas on the Stakes paid handsomely. *Hurry On* came in first. Holmes was back at his bee-farm on the Sussex South Downs. I was at the Queen Anne Street surgery, attending my well-to-do patients. More months went by. The adventure at Raffley Park faded from my mind until one morning a letter arrived, postmarked Folkestone.

Dear 'Mr. Wilson' (it read),

I foresee the end to this terrible war in England's favour cannot be too far off. Therefore I have chosen to escape back to my homeland. Soon the Kaiser will be forced into exile. I am posting this the very moment my feet once more walk upon my country's soil. I was received like a Wagnerian heroine in Berlin, and after some interrogation (which I passed satisfactorily!) posted to their front lines, Fourmies, thirty-one miles from Valenciennes, surrounded by forests and ponds, where German Intelligence suspected a 'nest of British spies' was at work. As it turned out, they were right. Soon I uncovered the nest, led, as it turned out, by a French childhood friend of mine, Felix (codenamed 'Dominique'). He and his wife and two young sisters lived in a cottage overlooking a railway line. Not only did I not give them away, I was able to keep their activities hidden from the Germans. On certain occasions I joined them. I must now be the only English woman <u>saboteure</u> who has actually put sand into axle-boxes.
Together, Felix and family worked in shifts twenty-four hours a day, watching for trains through a small slit in the heavy curtains, reporting the results to me. At one point, one-hundred-and-sixty trains per day went past. We

estimated a heavy Howitzer train would contain 6,000 150-millimeter rounds. I can assure you, not a single troop train passed unobserved, day or night. At the end of each shift, Felix made use of foodstuffs to keep tally on the number of trains and soldiers – beans for soldiers, coffee for guns, chicory for horses and so on. Felix and family (and I) survived, though several hundred of the others connected with train-watching were caught and imprisoned, and over one-hundred shot. The intelligence they obtained saved thousands of Allied lives. When we put the information on paper, we rolled the page up and tucked it inside the hollow handle of a broom standing in a corner of the kitchen. Then I sent it on in code with all possible speed to the War Office Secret Service via Colonel 'O', the British Military Attaché at The Hague.

The note ended: *The area has now been liberated from German occupation. I hope you and Mr. H and I will meet again, under more promising (and peaceful) circumstances. I shall be eternally grateful to you both for allowing me my life. I hope I have repaid our country for my stupidity and your kindness.*

DWF

P.S. I miss my evenings at the 'Who'd A Thought It'.

"*DWF*," I murmured, folding the letter. "*Die Weisse Frau.*" No mention of her German fiancé Ulrich – nor of the four dried violet leaves. It now seemed incredible that if Holmes had ordered me to shoot her, I would have done so with at most a moment's hesitation. She would have become the only woman I had ever killed, but spies are spies. The rules of war demanded it. Yet I admired how collected she had stayed that evening in her bunker, even in the face of immediate annihilation.

A week later another letter arrived, this time from Toby McCoy.

Dear Dr. Watson (it began),

I have had the most wonderful surprise. I've received a letter from Adrienne. You remember her? One of the girls in the knitting circle? Yes, that one! Then you'll also know, to everyone's bewilderment, no doubt yours and Mr. Holmes's as much as mine, she disappeared after the last airship attack. Until today I'd heard neither hide nor hair of her or her whereabouts. Her letter explains her nerves were stretched to the limit by the repeated Zeppelin attacks. After her first sting up North, she worried people would feel she was bringing bad luck on the Remount depots, so she took the lease on an abandoned cottage somewhere in the Lake District to recover (by reading Wordsworth, perhaps?). Now, with the war coming to a positive conclusion, she has decided to return to Wiltshire and would like to see me. (The words *like to see me* were heavily underlined.)

She asked if I was still a Second Lieutenant in the Intelligence Corps. I've replied already to say how delighted I will be, though rumour has it the Remount dépôts will be disbanded once the Armistice is signed. Already the girls at Raffley Park are planning their futures. Most want to marry well and settle down to family life and children. Some suffragette types want to go on to university. At least two want to try their hand at becoming jockeys. Although I'm sure with her family connections and all that, Adrienne wouldn't want to take up with someone like me (romantically I mean,) perhaps we might go into a training business together. She was easily the finest horsewoman here.

Fingers crossed!

Yours sincerely

Toby McCoy

I wrote back:

Dear Toby,

Any young lady should think it a privilege to marry a jockey who won the 2,000 Guineas at Newmarket! Make sure you invite Holmes and me to the wedding.

P.S. Is Ballymacad worth a five-guinea bet at the Gatwick Races?

I retrieved Adrienne's letter from a desk drawer and stared at it. My forehead wrinkled. Why choose to return before an armistice had been arranged? News from the Eastern Front indicated our ally Russia's resistance was weakening. If St. Petersburg withdrew from the fight, it would allow untold numbers of hardened German troops to flood back to the Western Front. In fact, according to my illustrious informer, the Rt. Hon. Sir George C., rumours abounded of a German spring offensive. The German High Command would soon give their Divisions the order to emerge like sewer rats from the Hindenburg trenches, the *Siegfriedstellung*, and make an irresistible assault on our defences, driving us back northward to the sea. Was Adrienne's chosen time to return simply a coincidence? Could her story about a childhood friend by the name of Felix ('Dominique') be complete rubbish? A fabrication? Or had I myself been reading too many of William Le Queux's spy stories of late? Would she want to return at the behest of the German High Command to become an enemy agent again, at yet another Army Remount depot under an assumed name?

I put the letter back in its drawer. The idea was ludicrous. On the other hand, she had made no mention of the love of her young life, Ulrich Hoffmeyer. What was *he* up to now?

The End

© Tim Symonds and Lesley Abdela 2018

NOTES

Given Holmes knowledge of the recondite, he probably knew the origin of Adrienne's code-name *Die Weisse Frau*, the legendary *White Lady* of the Hohenzollerns, a dynasty of former princes, electors, kings, and emperors of Hohenzollern, Brandenburg, Prussia, the German Empire, and Romania, a ghostly figure that walked about at night terrifying people. Her appearance was supposed to herald the downfall of the dynasty. It is said she has been seen on many occasions over hundreds of years, and linked to immediate deaths and disasters shortly after each dreadful sighting

'Room 40' refers to MI5 and SIS. Two agencies emerged from the split of the Secret Service Bureau in 1910 into domestic and overseas branches. One was MI5, the Security Service, *i.e.* the fifth department of the Directorate of Military Intelligence. It had an important role to play in tracking spies, in censorship, blockade operations, and penetrating enemy embassies in Britain.

The other was called MI1c, later SIS – *Secret Intelligence Service* – and later still MI6. The SIS worked in an occasionally fractious but generally productive collaboration with military intelligence overseas, producing vital information from agents and resistance networks on enemy war preparations and troop movements.

They had only begun to establish procedures and recruit staff before the Great War began. Some of the greatest advances were made in a field where there was virtually no capability before 1914, such as Signals Intelligence (SIGINT). Room 40 of the Admiralty (one of whose notable contributions was the decoding of the Zimmerman Telegram) and Section MI1b of the War Office together changed the British Intelligence landscape and laid the foundations for much of modern communications technology. (Information from *Secret Intelligence and British policy, 1909–45* by Gill Bennett. Foreign and Commonwealth Office, London)

Codebreaking ended up having a strong influence on the course of the war. As the Great War progressed, the race between codemaker and codebreaker accelerated, with combatants devising new and ever more devious ciphers, and their adversaries finding ways to crack them. His Majesty's Government really did ban the posting of knitting abroad, including knitting patterns, in case they contained coded messages. Code-making and code-breaking proved so important that by 1918, cryptologic organisations were no longer small groups of back-room 'boffins' but considerable bureaucracies increasingly integrated into normal military practice and operations.

The Germans too were not lagging. One curious incident is mentioned in Alan Judd's *The Quest For C*, where a well-dressed Belgian woman of good family, looks, and education who had good cause "to hate the Boche" was recruited by British Intelligence (possibly MI1c) to become a German double-agent. She bamboozled the Germans completely. She was sent by Berlin to Paris with 'several articles of underclothing impregnated with secret ink for delivery to a certain address'. Her work helped destroy the German spy network in neutral Switzerland. Unfortunately, the Germans didn't initiate her into how the ink was developed.

The real Ulrich Hoffmeyer was a friend of mine at university – despite the fact his father had been shot by the British for Nazi affiliations.

RECOMMENDED READING:

The Quest For C, by Alan Judd. Harper Collins.
Secret Service – The Making of The British Intelligence Community, by Christopher Andrew. Sceptre.

The Ghost of Dorset House

by Tim Symonds

At eight o'clock on an April evening in 1894 a ghost came upon an intruder in a great London mansion and chased him through pitch-black staterooms and corridors to his death. While this event was taking place, a hansom cab was returning me to my surgery in Kensington from a visit to a patient in the fashionable district of Knightsbridge. I stared sleepily out at the deserted gas-lit streets. To judge by our twists and turns, the cabbie was treating me to a tour of the townhouses of the nation's aristocracy – the Salisburys, the Derbys, the Devonshires. Devonshire House in particular was the site of the most exclusive social affairs, the centre of London's political life. A life from which I had been excluded since the death at the Reichenbach Falls three years earlier of my friend and comrade-in-arms, Mr. Sherlock Holmes, Europe's greatest Consulting Detective.

I took out my pocket-watch. Ten past eight. By the most direct route I would expect to reach my quarters by half-past, but an overturned Park Drag blocked the way ahead causing my driver to divert from Park Lane into Deanery Street. To the left stood a gate-keeper's lodge made of brick and heart pine. From it a drive led to a vast house shaped like a parallelogram, the grounds circled by a massive stone wall. Any thought I might have entertained of a pick-me-up nap over the last stretch of the journey was ended by a sudden burst of frantic shouting. A man, his face strained with fear, came rushing from the lodge, shouting "Police, police!" in a high, panicky voice.

I threw down the window and called out, "My dear fellow, what on earth's the matter?"

"Something's going on in the Great House, sir." He gasped. "There was a light inside when no-one's meant to be there. The light went out and crashings and screams began, screams so terrible, sir, it's hard to reconcile them with the order of Nature."

"And you are?" I enquired.

"Sykes, sir." He pointed at the brick and wood building behind him. "The lodge keeper."

"So, Sykes, you rushed up to the house at once?" I enquired in an ironic tone.

"No, sir, I did not," came the lodge keeper's petrified reply. "Not for a minute. The Master makes light of it, in fact he pooh-poohs it, but the staff say the house has become haunted. Not terrible screams like just now, but someone – more like *something* – straight from Hades, Lord preserve us, hurrying through the corridors and rooms at night for weeks now, its torso guttering like a lantern."

"Your Master being the Duke of Weymouth?" I asked, remembering the title of the ancient family who owned Dorset House, for that is where we were.

"Not the Duke, sir, no," the lodge keeper replied, his chest still heaving with fear. "The house is let to the American Ambassador to the Court of St. James. His name is Mr. Hammersmith. He occupies the house, but he's away. I've not seen 'ide nor 'air of him for three days. The house has been quite empty."

"What of the other staff?" I enquired.

"All away," came the reply. "The Master sent them away too. All 'cept me."

I stepped from the hansom, unhooking one of the carriage lamps.

"Lead on, my good fellow," I ordered the trembling lodge keeper. "The cabbie can fetch a constable. As to whether a doctor may be required, considering the ghastly screams and bangings you say you heard, I am myself a member of that profession. As such," I added, a trifle sententiously, "I'm not given to a belief in the Occult."

"*You* may not, sir," Sykes asserted, "but even famous men believe in things like ectoplasm and rappings and ghosts returning from the Other World. A demon from Hell, sir, is what we reckon it is. The cook's already packed up and gone back to Devon."

It was not unexpected to find the doors at the impressive main entrance firmly locked. A hard push indicated it was also bolted. We circled the outer walls until my companion exclaimed "There!" A window had been jemmied open. We entered and shortly came to a wide hallway running the length of the ground floor. A line of antique statues lay as though scythed down, terracotta heads and arms and legs scattered several feet from their torso. Just beyond, the shattered glass of an oil lamp glittered among glossy black shards of a Bucchero pot. A heavy inundation of blood commenced some five yards beyond the figurines, but not on the marble floor. Instead, it was a foot or so to the side of a wide doorway at a height of about five feet. Judging by the explosion of blood, the impact of the man's face on the wall had badly damaged the nasal mucosa.

The lodge keeper issued a low whistle.

"Someone must've banged him hard against that wall, sir," Sykes marvelled. "Who'd ever 'ave thought any man would have that much blood in 'im!"

A trail of bloody shoe marks commenced immediately beyond the door, crossing to the foot of a grand staircase. I had seen this particular configuration in Afghanistan, at the Battle of Maiwand. A bullet from a long arm Jezail rifle sent me reeling off the field in the arms of my orderly, my shoulder haemorrhaging blood, soaking my boots until they began to slip and slide on the surface of the rocks.

"Now that's interesting, sir," the lodge keeper exclaimed. "Despite doing all that smashing of statues back there, he's still trying to keep as quiet as possible. Look how he's tiptoeing along."

I replied tersely, "I doubt if the smashing was on purpose. And certainly he wasn't tip-toeing."

"Then why are there just toe-prints in the blood, sir?"

"Look at the length of his stride, man. The wretched fellow was running, running desperately, running for his life. He cannonaded willy nilly into those statues. His lamp smashed against the pot, but still he carried on at speed, even though – to judge by that wall – he must have been running in the pitch dark."

"So where do you reckon 'e is now?" my companion whispered.

"We'll follow the trail and find out," I replied.

Minutes later, Sykes's question was answered. A man lay motionless on the floor. In life he had been between fifty and sixty years of age. The face was split wide at several points across the forehead. The nose was badly broken. Around an outflung arm lay a scattering of jewellery.

"A thief all right," my companion muttered, his voice muted at the sight of death. "That pair of emerald cuff-links, them's Mr. Hammersmith's."

"You can turn on the lights now, Sykes," I ordered.

A switch clicked three or four times.

"They're not working," the lodge keeper called out.

I asked, "Would your Master have ordered the electricity to be turned off while he's away?"

"Never has before," came the reply. "Quite the contr'y. When the place is empty, he likes me to come up at night and check all's well. Not that I've done so lately," he added.

"Can you show me where the electricity enters the house?"

"I can, sir. We'll have to go back through that window. It's a bit to the left of it."

"One more thing before we go," I said. "The rings and the cuff-links...pick them up and hand them to me."

I stood over the dead man and let the handful of jewellery dribble out of my grasp. The spread was contained to within the original foot or two span of the outstretched hand.

We encountered Inspector MacDonald a few minutes later when I was clambering through the window to the outside, though it was his revolver I saw first. For several seconds he and I stared at each other. Noting the epaulettes, I broke the silence, "There's something you should see back there, Inspector."

The policeman's lamp came closer to my face.

"Good heavens!" he exclaimed with a slight Aberdonian lilt. "Why, it's Dr. Watson!" The inspector waved the revolver with a slightly embarrassed air and put it into a hidden holster.

"I'm gratified you recognise me, Inspector," I replied. "My cab was passing on my way home when Sykes here came running out of the lodge."

I pointed towards the now-invisible holster. "I didn't know our police were armed."

"Special duty, Doctor," came the friendly but non-committal reply. "There's a lot of very important people in this district, not least the prominent member of the *Corps Diplomatique* who lives in this house. Now tell me, what have you found in there? Cadavers galore?"

"Not galore, Inspector," I replied. "But certainly one cadaver."

From behind me the lodge keeper added emphatically, "A very dead cadaver. Blood everywhere."

"Before I take you to the body," I told MacDonald, "we must discover why the electricity isn't working in the house. Our friend here is about to show me the outside connection."

The lodge keeper led us forward and pointed at a waterproof box down low. "There, sirs. That's what they call the disconnect box. It's where the 'lectricity comes in from the big new station at Deptford East. The Duke of Weymouth always likes to be first with anything new."

"Hold back a moment, There's a good fellow, Sykes," the business-like inspector interrupted sharply. "Before anyone steps too close, someone get some light right over the box."

The lamps flooded two or three square yards of damp earth.

"See there, Dr. Watson," MacDonald said, "the wire's cut. Someone's been standing by the disconnect box with sacking over his shoes, and recently too. There are just flat impressions of the soles. I expect the corpse you found had sacking around his shoes?"

"No, Inspector," I replied.

"As you'll soon discover for yourself," Sykes added.

MacDonald stepped forward a pace. "You see!" he exclaimed, standing back with a tiny section of wire in his hand. "As I suspected. The cunning blighter. He didn't just yank the cable out of the socket. He cut an inch out of it to stop it being repaired too quickly."

I took the short piece of wire from him, turning it end to end.

"Why," I asked, "would a burglar need to cut the electricity off when it was clear the entire house was empty? A thief could find everything he wanted with just the lamp he'd have with him."

"That's a fair question, Doctor," MacDonald admitted. "Perhaps as a precaution?"

"Possibly," I agreed, "but at a considerable risk. At the very least it would indicate a burglary had taken place. A hunt would commence the minute anyone returned to the house."

"So why do you suppose it's been cut?" MacDonald continued. He pointed at the piece of wire in my hand. "Cut it certainly was."

"That's the question I believe our dear departed friend Sherlock Holmes would ask," I admitted, a momentary sadness overtaking me.

Inspector MacDonald threw me a sympathetic look.

"Bad deal about Mr. Holmes," he said.

I nodded. For readers in parts of the world so remote that even earth-shattering news never reaches them, I should explain that hardly three years earlier, my great friend Sherlock Holmes and I had been in the remote Alpine village of Meiringen when Holmes had finally encountered that greatest schemer of all time, the organiser of every deviltry, Professor James Moriarty, for a once-and-for-all showdown. Moriarty and Holmes grappled at a cliff edge before plunging into the boiling waters of the Reichenbach Falls, held for eternity in each other's iron grip. So died a friend and comrade-in-arms that I shall ever regard as the best and the wisest man I have ever known.

As though Holmes himself had prompted it, an idea flashed into my mind. I gesticulated urgently at the lodge keeper. "The burglar's tools, man. Where are they? He must have had a bag with him."

"You're right, sir, by the broken pot," Sykes responded. "There's a carpet-bag there."

"Quick," I said, "go and fetch it." I pointed at the severed wire. "It may well contain the answer to this."

Minutes later, the bag lay open at our feet. One by one, I took out a supply of burglar's tools – a small crowbar, a jemmy, a chisel, and a screwdriver, none showing any signs of wear – and last of all, the object of my search, a pair of wire-cutters. They had been lying at the very bottom of the bag. With the inspector and lodge keeper watching keenly, I snipped off a further quarter-inch from the piece of electric cable and held it up to a lamp.

"I think, Inspector," I said rather dramatically, "you'll see There's a difference between the two cuts. These pliers are sharp. They sliced through the cable. On the other hand, whoever cut the wire in the first place used a blunt pair of pliers. The wires were pretty well squeezed apart, not cut. Those well-worn pliers were the ones which cut off the electricity."

"Meaning…?" asked Inspector MacDonald.

"It was done by someone who wanted the intruder inside the mansion with no electricity."

"But why?" MacDonald queried. The Aberdonian accent was growing stronger, as though he was about to break into Doric.

"Answer that, my dear Inspector," I replied, "and we are a long way towards solving this mystery."

It was time to take Inspector MacDonald to the shattered figurines and onwards to the corpse. On our way, I pointed out the trail of scarlet shoe-prints.

"Inspector, look at each step. There's just the toe of the shoe marked out in blood, the intruder's own blood. He started to flee for his life, and he continued even after his lantern was dashed to the ground, leaving him in complete darkness. A panic of the highest order must have caused him to continue at such speed, even though he was crashing into walls and cannonading off staircases. At all costs, he had to get away from something utterly terrible."

I held my lantern close to the marble floor. "As you'll note, there's a second person present. He's the one with cladding over his shoes. He must have cut the electricity."

"Then, Dr. Watson," queried the inspector, "if the second man was pursuing him, why didn't they grapple with each other? There's no sign of a struggle."

"Because," I replied, "the pursuer had no intention of seizing him. Inspector, you have been an avid reader of my stories in *The Strand*?"

"Every one of them, Doctor, without fail, I can assure you," came the reply.

"Then let me test your powers of recall. In which of Holmes's cases did I write: '*There was one thing in the case which had made the deepest impression both upon the servants and the police. This was the contortion of the Colonel's face. It had set, according to their account, into the most dreadful expression of fear and horror which a human countenance is capable of assuming*'."

At this the inspector broke in with "'*More than one person fainted at the mere sight of him, so terrible was the effect*'. Why, Doctor, that's easy! 'The Adventure of the Crooked Man'."

I bent down and turned the corpses head towards him. "Take a look at this man's face," I ordered. "As you will see, it could hardly be more contorted from terror." I turned to the silent lodge keeper. "Sykes, would you say we're five or six rooms from the shattered lamp?"

"Six, yes, sir. From just this side of the state rooms. Them's down that end of the house, Inspector, near the room the Master uses for his private study."

"Whoever chased this wretched creature could easily have grabbed hold of him a long way before they reached here," I continued. "There's one more thing of note, Inspector. Whoever or whatever was chasing him wasn't holding a lamp, or at least it wasn't lit. Otherwise, his quarry – only a yard or two in front of him – would hardly have crashed into walls or tripped up stairways. The two of them hurtled along in the pitch black, the one just behind the other..." I pointed down at the corpse. "...but only the one was cannonading into walls and door-jambs."

"The phantom, sir!" the lodge keeper cried. "*Now* do you believe...?"

"Sykes," I interrupted sharply, "I hope my cabbie has been good enough to wait for me. Would you be kind enough to return to the street? Tell him I expect to be there in a few minutes. Don't provide him with any lurid details, only that we have found a body. Do you understand?"

MacDonald asked, "If the pursuer could have grappled with him at any time, how do you explain the distance they ran?"

"Capturing the intruder wasn't top of his priorities. What else would explain it? He wanted him to reach such a pitch of terror this man's heart or brain would explode. I believe the autopsy will show the pursuer achieved his grisly aim wonderfully well."

"Just like the case of Sir Charles and the Hound of the Baskervilles?" the inspector asked, a rather disbelieving twinkle in his eye. "Everyone at the Yard has heard of the Hound."

"Exactly like the Hound," I replied. "Such intense fear as I believe our cadaver here suffered in his last moments alive can cause a disorganised heart movement, a quiver. Not the regular beat required to sustain life. Driving someone to their death this way is as much murder as firing a bullet through the vital organs."

I turned to face MacDonald head on. "Now, Inspector, I expect you've already come to a conclusion? That something took place here quite unique in the annals of crime?"

He shook his head. "On the contrary, Doctor. I'm baffled. Unique in the annals of crime, you say? I can't hold with Sykes's theory of a ghost, though the idea of being chased all that way in the utter dark has got me a bit spooked, I must admit."

I replied, trying hard not to appear triumphal, "Let me remind you of one of my friend Sherlock Holmes's favourite axioms: *"How often have I said to you that when you have eliminated the impossible, whatever remains, however improbable, must be the truth?"*

The bushy eyebrows were raised. "And what might that truth be?"

"At least you and I appear to agree on one fundamental," I parried.

71

"Which is?"

"This is not the work of some Risen Dead, as Sykes is inclined to believe."

"I think I can accept that, Doctor," came the smiling reply. "And then?"

"The living being who perpetrated this dastardly deed knew exactly which way the dead man would have to flee – towards this or that door, along this or that corridor. His knowledge of the house must have been extensive. Inch-for-inch, in fact."

"I'll go along with that, yes. Next?"

"The pursuer took care to have a handful of Hammersmith's jewellery at the ready."

"Why in heaven's name would he do that?" MacDonald exclaimed.

"To salt the corpse. Look at the close spread of the jewellery. When a man crashes to the marble floor the pieces should be flung from his grasp far and wide. Instead, we found them more or less as you see them now, contained to within a foot or two of his hand."

"Very good. And?"

"Last but very far from least, the murderer has a characteristic which neither the dead man, nor you nor I nor Sykes, have in common with him, a condition normally considered a disability, but one without which his fiendish plan may have ended in complete failure."

The eyebrows rose even higher.

"A *disability*?"

"A vital one," I affirmed.

"There's no evidence he was lame."

"Not lame," I replied.

"Then?"

"Blind."

There was a moment's astonished silence before Inspector MacDonald emitted the loudest guffaw I had ever heard.

His hand reached out and gripped my arm, his shoulders heaving. "My dear Doctor," he gasped finally, "I assume this fellow Sykes told you?"

"Told me what?" I asked, taken aback by this unexpected reaction.

"Or did I tell you back there on the terrace? Though I don't recall doing so, but perhaps I did!"

"Inspector, you or Sykes may have told me *what?*" I persisted.

"Why, the only blind person around here is the American Ambassador himself!" and once more MacDonald went off into a paroxysm of laughter. "I hope," he spluttered, "you aren't suggesting it was the Ambassador himself who chased the housebreaker from here to Kingdom Come!"

We returned in silence to the back terrace.

"If he's the only blind man in the household," I recommenced, "then, yes, I point the finger at the Ambassador, Inspector. He would know how to find his way unfailingly through every door and up and down every staircase in the pitch dark, avoiding any obstacles – even Etruscan statues – on the way. Sykes told me a demonic figure has been glimpsed running through the corridors and rooms in the dark of night for the past several weeks, *'its torso guttering like a lantern'*. The staff were frightened enough to plan to quit *en masse*. I suggest it was the Ambassador practicing for the events of this evening."

"My dear Doctor Watson," MacDonald replied, wiping tears of laughter from his eyes, "even if you are right, it's entirely conjecture. *'Its torso guttering like a lantern'*, you say. What of proof? If I take in the Ambassador of a friendly State for questioning on what we have here, I'll become the laughing stock of the Force. My chances of rising through the ranks will be rather less than zero. I'd find myself running an alehouse in the Out Skerries. No, I'm afraid that at best I'm going to have to report death by misadventure, certainly not *malum in se*. What's more, I think we'll find the denizens of every grand house around Mayfair saying 'Well done and good riddance' at the demise of anyone caught stealing their valuables or family heirlooms, even at the hands of a ghost."

Courteously MacDonald saw me back to my carriage.

I was within a quarter-mile of my residence when the driver rapped on the roof.

"I was just thinking, sir," he called down. "You asked me back there if I'd seen anyone hurrying out of the grounds while you were up in the big house."

"And you replied no-one, except Sykes delivering my message to you."

"I did indeed say no-one, sir. But you didn't ask me if anyone *come* to the lodge, did you, sir?"

"I did not," I agreed. "And did they?"

"They did. A growler comes speeding around the corner from the direction of South Audley Street. The cabbie jumps down and takes a box pushed out from the cab itself. He drops it at the lodge door, clambers straight up on the Clarence, and off they shoot. Gone in a second. If I'd got a better sight of him, I'd report him for whipping the horses like he did. I went over and took a gander at the box when Mr. Sykes fetched it in. It was marked Diplomatic Bag. There was a seal attached to it."

"Cabbie!" I shouted out. "Return us immediately to Dorset House. Quick, man! Get us back there within fifteen minutes and there's an extra guinea in it for you."

The lodge keeper opened the door. It was clear he was still distraught. I had to repeat my question before he pulled himself together.

"A box, sir?"

"A diplomatic bag," I said. "Sealed. It arrived when we were up at the house."

"Ah, that one, sir," came the reply. "It's over there, among the other Diplomatic bags. They arrive any time of the day or night. Look at 'em – cardboard boxes, briefcases, crates. All sealed."

"Open the new arrival!" I cried.

"Sir!" the lodge keeper protested. "Only the Ambassador hisself is allowed to break the seals!"

I said sharply. "If we are to solve this bizarre crime you must open the bag. Open it at once, man. Otherwise I shall hold you responsible for letting the trail go cold."

The lodge keeper broke the seal. I bent down and lifted out a piece of blood-stained sacking.

"Well, I'm damned," a now-familiar voice spoke behind me. It was Inspector MacDonald.

I held out the sacking. "This is what he wrapped around his shoes, Inspector. It not only prevented us from comparing his shoes to the imprints outside, but it meant he was utterly silent as he chased his victim around the house. And," I continued, reaching down to retrieve an elderly pair of wire-cutters, "I think we know what these were used for."

I lifted out the final item, a black garment tailored to fit a man of about six feet in height from head to toe. Daubed on it in luminous paint, flickering like a thousand glow-worms, were the bones and skull of a human skeleton.

"Inspector, we live in an age when a white sheet and some dark shadows are quite enough to frighten even the most cosmopolitan victim to death. This outfit was as effective as if he'd taken a new Army & Navy Colt and blown the intruder's brains out."

MacDonald's brows knitted. "Well," he said cautiously. "I think we may have enough. The Met will be appreciative, Dr. Watson, I'm sure about that. You, Sykes, take some wax and

75

reseal the box and its contents. Say nothing to anyone about it. Do I make myself clear? I'll want to know if the Ambassador himself seems especially keen to collect it."

The cabbie drove me home. Jubilant as I was, a sad thought recurred time and again over the journey. If only Holmes had been alive to hear a blow by blow account of how I helped MacDonald solve the murder. Alas, my old friend's bones were entangled for ever with those of Moriarty, the 'Napoleon of Crime', in some *danse macabre* at the foot of those distant Falls.

Epilogue

In view of the inspector's words when we parted, the reader may imagine my dismay and irritation when, two days later, tucked deep in the inner pages of *The Daily Telegraph*, I read:

> *Burglary in Mayfair – A string of burglaries may now come to an end with the discovery of the corpse of a house-thief within the premises of a grand house in Mayfair. 'Swag' in the form of valuable jewellery was found at his side. He was pronounced dead by a passing doctor. The deceased's clothing gave no clues as to his identity. No relative has come forward to claim the body. Scotland Yard Inspector Alec MacDonald told* The Telegraph, *"Any premature death is an unfortunate occurrence but we are confident the recent spate of burglaries near Dorset House will now cease."*

A week later, the departure of the American Ambassador was widely reported, '*a popular figure among the* Corps Diplomatique, *whose blindness proved no impediment to the successful commission of his duties.*'

Ambassador Hammersmith, it was explained, had decided to return to the United States of America after being "deeply disturbed" by the recent discovery of the body of a burglar in the house he occupied on Deanery Street, London.

I flung the newspaper to one side. '*He was pronounced dead by a passing doctor*' hardly described the role I had played. I cancelled my day's patients and went for an extended walk to overcome my disappointment. Even a common-or-garden burglar deserved justice.

Twelve years passed before I was to discover what truly lay behind the death of the intruder. The case had been curious enough though in retrospect I was myself inclined to laugh (albeit grimly) at some of its grotesque and fantastical features.

I was on my way for a constitutional in Regents Park when threatening clouds diverted me to the Junior United Services Club, where I could spend a convivial hour in the dry with commissioned officers past and present, above all those of the 19th Punjabi and the 28th Indian Cavalry. Instead, the first person to catch my eye was MacDonald. He was seated alone, chin on hands, his great sandy eyebrows bunched into a yellow tangle. At his side lay two or three folders. I was beckoned over with a friendly wave.

"Thank goodness for a familiar face!" he exclaimed. "I confess I feel like a sore thumb sticking out among all these senior officers."

A would-be host had as yet failed to materialise.

I pointed at the insignia of rank on his shoulders, a crown above a Bath Star, known as 'pips', over crossed tipstaves within a wreath. It was very similar to the insignia worn by a full general in the British Army.

"I read of your promotion to Commissioner of Police of the Metropolis, MacDonald. Congratulations."

"In no small part due to you, Doctor," he replied in his still-evident Aberdonian accent. "I became a man marked out for promotion the moment you solved the Dorset House murder for me."

My forehead furrowed. "But you reported it as a mere burglary. It didn't even rate a snippet in the *Police Gazette*."

"Paradoxically, because it turned out to be the most important case Special Branch had worked on for years! Every editor in Britain was ordered in no uncertain terms not to print a word."

I caught the eye of a steward. "What's your tipple, Commissioner?"

"Whisky would be nice."

An unexpected silence fell upon our conversation. My companion gnawed a thumb, staring at me thoughtfully. At one point he surreptitiously ran a hand over a side-pocket.

The drinks arrived. MacDonald leaned forward.

"I'm not in a position to tell you precisely why, Dr. Watson, but it's extraordinarily fortuitous to meet you like this. First, remind me, have you signed the 1889 Official Secrets Act?"

"I have," I replied.

"Then you'll especially recall Section One (c), *'where a person after having been entrusted in confidence by some officer under Her Majesty the Queen with any document, sketch, plan, model, or information'* ...continue please!"

"*'...wilfully and in breach of such confidence communicates the same when, in the interest of the State, it ought not to be communicated'*. I do indeed," I replied, smiling at the officialdom. "Does this mean you're about to tell me more about the Ghost of Dorset House?"

"I am, yes. A great deal of water has flowed under the bridge. You'll find what I am about to reveal to you a very pretty matter indeed. You know Ambassador Hammersmith is dead? Trampled by a bison he kept as a pet."

Over a generous tot of fine Glen Garrioch, Commissioner MacDonald went on to fill in with remarkable detail matters of which I had known nothing.

"The Ambassador," he began, "was a born and bred American, but a direct descendant of Junkers, members of the higher *edelfrei* nobility. At some point, his paternal line adopted the name Hammerschmidt. On arrival at Ellis Island, the father's name was anglicised by an immigration official and became Hammersmith. The son's loyalties, second to his native land, America, grew attached to the young and intemperate Kaiser Wilhelm. The American developed a great deal of sympathy for the German Emperor's hatred of the British Empire."

"Are you saying the Ambassador was a threat to England's safety?" I asked.

"More than you would ever guess," he replied gravely, "but we'll return to that in a moment. It seems Hammersmith had come to believe he was being watched by the British Government. Over the three months leading up to the events of that night, he had reported several break-ins. Petty thefts – silverware, some cash, that sort of thing. The claims explain why I was on the spot so quickly. I was on permanent watch in the neighbourhood. Despite my vigil, no-one was apprehended. In retrospect, we can see the thefts were entirely imaginary, but cleverly designed to influence the authorities. He was setting up the scene for the murder. The police coming to investigate the mysterious death of an intruder would readily assume the corpse was a cat-burglar who'd tried his luck at Dorset House once too often and met his come-uppance.

"At most, the coroner would register it as an unexplained death and leave it at that. Hardly a week goes by in any of our big cities where someone isn't found dead in the course of carrying out some crime or other – falling off a roof, tumbling down a steep flight of stairs. The Ambassador must have thought he could get away with murder without the slightest suspicion falling on him, and I have to say, Doctor, had you not been passing by at that moment, that would have been the most likely outcome. None of us would ever have concluded a blind man could be the murderer. As it was, that was your remarkable deduction. The discovery of the skeleton suit confirmed it. The moment your carriage sped on its way, I called in a dozen colleagues from Special Branch. We reconnected the electricity and went through the house with a tooth-comb."

As he spoke he reached into a pocket and withdrew a small wooden box about an inch by one-and-a-half inches.

"We found this under a stairwell." He passed it across.

"A miniature camera?" I asked, turning it over and over.

"A bespoke camera developed for Special Branch by the camera-makers J. H. Dallmeyer. I brought it with me today in relation to another appointment, but I think that you should have it, Doctor. It has a completely silent shutter and a special lens for close up copy work. The dead man was probably using it at the very moment the 'phantom' rushed in on him, but being blind, the Ambassador wouldn't have known."

I stared from the camera to the Commissioner in bemusement. I began, "Why would a burglar have a ...?" Once again, as though Holmes were hovering at my side, the answer came to me: "You mean the victim wasn't a simple sneak-thief after all?"

My companion slapped a hand on his thigh in pleasure. "He was from Special Branch!" he cried. "The nation's security was entrusted to him. Special Branch had their suspicions about the Ambassador's repeated use of diplomatic channels to contact Berlin. Unknown to me, they put a man on to watching Dorset House, observing who came and went. Our chap knew his job. Not once did I catch sight of him. Then Hammersmith was seen driving out in his automobile, followed by a Clarence containing several pieces of expensive luggage. The servants departed soon afterwards, each carrying enough possessions to keep themselves in clothes for several days. The house was left completely dark. An opportunity to enter the mansion had presented itself. That's when the decision was taken to break in. Who could have known it was a cunning trap!"

MacDonald pulled out a rolled-up photograph. "Take a look at this," he urged, handing it across. "He only had time to take two snaps but they provided the proof we needed. Hammersmith was providing Germany with copies of top-secret documents of international importance. The one in the photograph shows the likely deployment of the Royal Navy's Ironclads in a first encounter with the Kaiser's High Seas Fleet if Berlin proved stupid enough to challenge Britain's vast naval power."

I passed the photograph back. "You mentioned a second snap?"

MacDonald looked around cautiously and showed me a second photograph. "This one's of a document *from* Berlin. It's the most egregious of all."

"A plot to kill the Parliamentary and Financial Secretary to the Admiralty!" I gasped. "My Heavens, MacDonald, surely that would have provided a *casus belli*?"

"If the assassination attempt had succeeded, no doubt it would," the Commissioner agreed. He pointed at the photograph.

"Thanks to this, we were able to thwart the plot. If our poor colleague had lived, he'd have been awarded a gong in Her Majesty's Birthday Honours, that's for sure." What was more, the Commissioner continued, a warrant to search Dorset House revealed more stolen and copied documents under the floor-boards, "and this little curiosity". He passed across a file titled *The History of Hammersmith District*. It contained a yellowing newspaper clipping dated late November 1803, some ninety years earlier than the events of that night. Somebody was roaming the nocturnal streets and lanes in a white sheet.

> *One night a heavily pregnant woman was crossing near the churchyard about ten o'clock... when she beheld*

81

something…rise from the tomb-stones. The figure was very tall, and very white! She attempted to run, but the ghost soon overtook her, and pressing her in his arms, she fainted. Found hours later by neighbours, she was put to bed in a state of shock and died there.

Commissioner MacDonald said, "You were right, Doctor. His intention was to frighten our man to death. And that must be where he got the idea."

"My heavens, MacDonald," I cried. "Adding all this up, it must have been dynamite! But the newspapers said the Ambassador took voluntary retirement? He wanted to spend more time on his buffalo ranch in Utah."

"Not exactly voluntary, Doctor. The Prime Minister passed the evidence to the American President. Within twenty-four hours, Hammersmith had to pack up his goods and chattels and was gone. He 'retired' from the Diplomatic Corps soon afterwards."

I recalled the photograph in *The Times*, a smiling Ambassador boarding the *Majestic* for the Atlantic crossing.

"There was no way we could charge the fellow in a British Court, but that didn't stop Her Majesty's Government declaring him *persona non grata*," MacDonald continued. "My report was received with relief in the highest quarters of the land. Special Branch was glad to see the back of him. It put an end to a very troublesome thorn in England's side." Leaning closer, he whispered, "It wasn't long before I found myself up for a significant promotion." He gestured at the pips on his shoulders. "You can see I haven't looked back since. I've a very great deal to thank you for."

As he uttered these words, behind his back I saw the steward directing an apologetic looking man towards MacDonald's leather armchair. I recognised the visitor at once, the holder of a very high public office.

I thrust the camera into a pocket and stood up. I lent forward and whispered, "I shall go now, Commissioner. This has been a most exceptional half-an-hour. I have just deduced you must be here to brief our recent Foreign Secretary, now Prime Minister, on Hammersmith's shenanigans, or you would not have had such an archive with you, let alone the camera."

The Commissioner's face turned ashen. "Good Lord, Doctor Watson, how on earth did you…?"

I replied, "Elementary, my dear MacDonald! To judge by his expression, an approaching Prime Minister is about to apologise to you for being so tardy, but I am entirely indebted to whichever matter of State it was that kept him."

I patted my pocket. "And who knows what Sherlock Holmes and I might get up to with this treasure of a camera."

The End

The Mystery of the Missing Artefacts

by Tim Symonds

August 1916

A dungeon under the Dolmabahçe Palace, Constantinople

I stared up at the patch of blue sky visible through a tiny grille high up on the wall. I was a prisoner-of-war in Constantinople, left to rot in a dank cell under the magnificent State Rooms of Sultan Mehmed V Reşâd. My only distraction was a much-thumbed copy of Joseph Conrad's *The Secret Agent*. Near-permanent pangs of hunger endlessly recalled a fine meal I enjoyed with my old friend Sherlock Holmes at London's famous Grand Cigar Divan restaurant some years earlier. What I would now give for such a repast, I reflected unhappily. Every detail came to mind: the Chef walking imposingly alongside the lesser mortal propelling a silver dinner wagon. Holmes ordering slices of beef carved from a large joint, I the smoked salmon, a signature dish of the establishment. For dessert, we decided upon the famous treacle sponge with a dressing of Madagascan vanilla custard. And a Trichinopoly cigar to top it off.

I should explain how twists and turns of fate had brought me to my present state. I shall not go into exhaustive detail. Suffice it to say that at the start of the war against the German Kaiser and his Ottoman ally I volunteered to rejoin my old Regiment. The Army Medical Corps assigned me to the 6th (Poona) Division of the British Indian Army which had captured the town of Kut-al-Amara a hundred miles south of Baghdad, in the heart of Mesopotamia. I had hardly taken up my post when the Sultan retaliated by ordering his troops to besiege us.

Five desperate months left us entirely without food or potable water. Our Commanding Officer surrendered. The victors separated British Field Officers from Indian Other Ranks and transported us to various camps across the Ottoman Empire. I found myself delivered to the very palace where ten years earlier the previous ruler, Sultan Abd-ul-Hamid II, received Sherlock Holmes and me as honoured guests.[1] Now I was confined to a dungeon under the two hundred and eighty five rooms, forty-six halls, six *hamams*, and sixty-eight toilets of the magnificent building of the Yildiz Palace. It was clear from the despairing cries of my fellow captives that I was to be left in squalor and near-starvation until the Grim Reaper came to take me to a Life Beyond.

The heavy door of my cell swung open. Rather than the surly Turkish warder bringing a once-daily bowl of watery grey soup, a visitor from the outside world stood there. We stared at each other. I judged him to be an American from the three-button jacket with long rolling lapels and shoulders free of padding. The four-button cuffs and military high-waisted effect reflected the influence of the American serviceman's uniform on civilian fashion.

The visitor spoke first. "Captain Watson M.D., I presume?" he asked cordially. He had a New England accent.

"At your service," I said warily, getting to my feet. I was embarrassed by the tattered state of my British Indian Army uniform and topee. "And you might be?"

Hand outstretched, the visitor stepped into the cell. "Mr. Philip," he replied. "American Embassy. A Diplomatic Courier came from England with a telegram for you. I apologise for the time it's taken to discover your whereabouts. At the American Embassy we are all acquainted with the crime stories in *The Strand* magazine written by Sherlock Holmes's great friend, Dr. John H. Watson. None of us realised the Ottoman prisoner of war 'Captain' Watson was one and the same." The emissary's gaze flickered around, suppressing any change of expression at the fetid air. The pestilential hole had been my home-from-home for more than a month. "Not the finest quarters for a British officer, are they?" he smiled sympathetically.

I pointed impatiently at the small envelope in his hand. "Is that the telegram?" I prompted. Mr. Philip handed it over with a nod. The envelope carried the words '*From Sherlock Holmes, for the Attention of Captain Watson M.D., Constantinople. To be delivered by hand.*'

"I have no doubt," Mr. Philip went on, "that it's to inform you your old companion is working energetically through the Powers-that-Be to have you released and returned to England."

Nodding agreement I tore open the envelope and read the contents. My jaw dropped. I glanced up at my visitor and returned my disbelieving gaze to the telegram. "*My dear Watson,*" I read again, "*Do you remember the name of the fellow at the British Museum who contacted us over a certain matter just before I retired to my bee-farm in the South Downs?*"

I remembered the matter in considerable detail. Towards the end of 1903, a letter marked *Urgent & Confidential* arrived at Holmes's Baker Street quarters. It was from a Michael Lacey, Keeper of Antiquities at the British Museum. Some dozens of small items in the Ancient and Mediaeval Battlefield department had gone missing, artefacts ploughed up on ancient battlegrounds or retrieved from graves of tenth or eleventh Century English knights and bowmen. The items were of no intrinsic value. The artefacts had spent some years in storage awaiting archiving, but due to a shortage of experts no work had been carried out. Would Mr. Holmes come to see the Keeper at the Museum and investigate their disappearance? At the time Holmes was dismissive. "Probably an inside job – perhaps a floor-sweeper hoping to augment a pitiful salary. It would hardly prove even a one-Abdulla-cigarette problem." My comrade had then clambered to his feet, reached for his Inverness cape and announced, "I plan to spend today at my bee-farm on the Sussex Downs, checking my little workers are doing what Nature designed for them, filling jars with a golden liquid purloined from the buttercup, the poppy, and the Blue Speedwell."

He looked back from the door. "Watson, don't look so crestfallen. It's hardly as if the umbra of Professor Moriarty of evil memory has marched in and stolen the Elgin Marbles. Kindly inform this Keeper of Antiquities that I haven't the faintest interest in the matter. Refer him to any Jack-in-office at Scotland Yard." His voice floated back up from the stairwell. "No doubt Inspector Lestrade will happily take time away from chasing horse-flies in Surrey to check on an owl job of such little consequence." With a shout to our landlady of "Good day, Mrs. Hudson!" Holmes stepped into the bustle of Baker Street and was gone.

Now, inexplicably, ten and more years later into retirement, he wanted to know the man's name. Not one word on my desperate situation. I turned the telegram over and wrote, *"Dear Holmes, the name of the Keeper at the British Museum was Michael Lacey. Why do you ask? I recall how rudely you refused to take up the case. You said that after 'A Scandal in Bohemia', no ordinary burglary could ever be of interest to you."* With blistering sarcasm I added, *"Would you do me a small favour? When you can find a moment away from whatever you're pursuing, get me out of here as quickly as possible? If the rancid slop doesn't do for me, cholera will."*

The days passed with agonising slowness. At last Mr. Philip returned. He told me the American Ambassador would shortly be making a demarche to the Sublime Porte to get me released. He handed me a second communication from England. I wrenched it open. The envelope contained a cutting from a Sussex newspaper, *The Battle Observer*. Below an advertisement for the Central Picture Theatre (*The Folly of Youth*), Holmes had marked out a photograph of a corpse lying in a field below ancient ruins. The photograph was attributed to a Brian Hanson, using a Sinclair Una De Luxe No. 2 – a camera I was myself planning to purchase using the savings from my Army pay, the single benefit from my enforced incarceration. The headline blared '*Strange Death of Former British Museum Keeper*'.

The report continued:

> *Early this morning, a body was discovered by local resident Mrs. Johnson, walking her dog across the site of the Battle of Hastings. An arrow jutted out of the deceased's left eye. The dead man has been identified as Michael Lacey, former Head of Antiquities at the British Museum. The police were called and the body removed to the Union Workhouse hospital. It is not known what the deceased was doing in the field in the night. It is a spot seldom frequented after dark. Local legend holds the land runs crimson with blood when the rain falls. Ghostly figures have made appearances – phantom monks and spectral knights, red and grey ladies. Furthermore, each October, on the eve of the famous battle, a lone ghostly knight has been reported riding soundlessly across the battlefield.*

The article ended with:

> *The police describe Mr. Lacey as a well-known if controversial and isolated figure. He has lived in the area since his retirement ten years ago to a house on Caldbec Hill. He was rumoured to hold to the widely-discredited theory that the Battle between William of Normandy and Harold Godwinson of England did not take place on the slopes below the present-day ruins of Battle Abbey but at a location several miles away. What remains certain is that William's victory and Harold's death from an arrow in the eye changed the course of our Island's history, laws, and customs.*

An accompanying note in Holmes's scrawl said, '*Come soonest. SH.*'

Finally *Kismet* rather than Holmes or the American Embassy came to my rescue. A Turkish Major-General fell into the hands of British forces outside Jerusalem. A prisoner-exchange was agreed. By early October, I was back in London, greeting the locum at my Marylebone surgery. In a matter of hours, the Chinese laundry on Tottenham Court Road restored my Indian Army uniform, topee, and Sam Browne belt to pristine condition. I would wear the uniform for my visit to Holmes to avoid the attention of the ladies of the Order of the White Feather.

I tarried further in the Capital just long enough to purchase a supply of black hothouse grapes from Solomon's in Piccadilly, and to visit Salmon and Gluckstein of Oxford Street where I stocked up with a half-a-dozen tins of J&H Wilson No. 1 Top Mill Snuff and several boxes of Trichinopoly cigars. The train deposited me at Eastbourne. I boarded a sturdy four-wheeler to engage with the mud.

Holmes's bee-farm was tucked in rolling chalk downland with close-cropped turf and dry valleys. Some miles later the lonely, low-lying black-and-white building with a stone courtyard and crimson ramblers came into view. Holmes was waiting to greet me. At the familiar sight a wave of nostalgia washed through me.

While I fumbled for money to pay the cabman, Holmes drummed his fingers on the side of the carriage. Payment made, at a touch of the driver's whip the horses wheeled and turned away. Holmes reached a hand across to my shoulder. "Well done, Watson," he said, adding in the sarcastic tone of old, "Prompt as ever in answering a telegraphic summons."

"Holmes!" I protested, "you might remember I was rotting in a dungeon in the Sultan's Palace two-thousand miles away when your invitation arrived. I was lucky to find a British warship in Alexandria, or I might have been incarcerated a second time. The Mediterranean bristles with the Kaiser's dreadnoughts and battle-cruisers."

To mollify me Holmes said, "We must ask my housekeeper, Mrs. Keppler, to bring you a restorative cup of tea. You will be offered a very civilised choice of shiny black tea or scented green."

We seated ourselves in the Summer-house. I handed over the tray of Solomon's black grapes and a share of the Trichinopoly cigars as gifts to my host. My comrade passed across a large copy of the newspaper picture I had first seen in the Turkish cell. "I obtained this at a modest charge from *The Battle Observer*," he explained. "Now, Watson, you're a medical chap. I need your help. My knowledge of anatomy is accurate, but unsystematic. Tell me, what do you think?"

"Think about what precisely?" I queried, staring at the corpse in the picture.

"The arrow in his eye, of course," came Holmes's reply. "The local police say he must have done it to himself. King Harold was shot in the eye by a Norman arrow. They suggest Lacey chose to die the same death, maddened by his failure to disprove the true site of the historic battle." He added, "The citizens of the town are in a hurry to close the case. They most definitely do not wish for unfavourable publicity ahead of the commemorative events."

"Which events?" I asked.

"The eight-hundred-and-fiftieth anniversary of the Battle of Hastings," Holmes replied. "In a week's time. Hundreds of visitors are expected. *Le Tout-Battle* wishes to make a lot of money from them."

"If you mean did the arrow cause Lacey's death, I can answer that straight away, Holmes. No, the arrow was not the cause of death. The angle of entry is quite wrong. It would have slipped past any vital part of the brain. In Afghanistan, I administered to one of our Indian troops who caught an arrow in the eye. He lived on for months and probably years."

"Could it have been self-inflicted?" Holmes asked.

"Unlikely," I replied. "In my opinion, he was already dead when the arrow was pushed into his eye."

Holmes asked, "So the fear and horror on his face?"

"Already frozen into it."

"Therefore the real cause of death?"

"Undoubtedly a heart attack," I replied. "From fright," I opined. "Something spine-chilling must have happened to this Lacey on that isolated spot. Whatever it was, a rush of adrenaline stunned his cardiac muscle into inaction. Think of Colonel Barclay's death in the matter of the Crooked Man. *He* died of fright. There's a close similarity here." I went on, "Dying of fright is a rather more frequent medical condition than you may imagine. I estimate one person a day dies from it in any of our great cities."

Holmes stood up. "You have me intrigued, Watson. We must hurry. Drink up your tea. I may not have displayed the slightest interest in the Keeper of Antiquities and his little problems while he was alive, but in death he presents a most unusual case."

"Hurry where?" I asked, bewildered.

"Why, to the British Museum, where else! It'll be like old times.

Within the quarter-hour a carriage arrived. As we jolted along, Holmes pulled out a packet of Pall Mall Turkish cigarettes and lit one, eyes narrowing against the smoke. He reached into his voluminous coat for the photographic print. He stared at the image, puffing in thoughtful silence. "What is it, Holmes?" I asked at last. "Why the knitted brow and repeated drumming on your knee?"

"There's something odd here, Watson. Something I quite missed at first. You have my copy of *The Observer* in your side-pocket. Can you pass it to me, please?" Holmes reached once more into his coat, withdrawing a ten-power silver-and-chrome magnifying glass. For a while it hovered over the newspaper. I was irresistibly reminded of a well-trained foxhound dashing back and forth through the covert, whining in its eagerness, until it comes across the lost scent.

Holmes gave a grunt. He passed the print and magnifying glass to me. "Tell me what you see," he ordered. I stared at the photograph through the powerful glass.

"Nothing unusual, Holmes," I said, looking up.

Holmes asked, "What about the grass under the corpse's head?"

"The ground around the body gives no indication of a deadly struggle," I replied. "Is that what you mean?"

He commanded, "Now look again at the grass around the body as it appears in *The Observer.*"

Once more I looked through the magnifying glass. "Why, it's nowhere near as clear as in the print, Holmes," I replied. "In fact it's quite grainy."

"Precisely, Watson. Why would the grass be quite clearly defined in the print but look grainy when the same photograph appears in the newspaper? This is a three-pipe problem at the very least, Watson. I beg you not to speak to me for fifty minutes."

Holmes flicked the cigarette butt out of the carriage window and produced his favourite blackened briar. I threw my tobacco pouch to his side and looked quickly out of the carriage window, blinking away a tear of happiness. The Sherlock Holmes of yesteryear was back.

After only one pipe, Holmes pointed at my Indian Army uniform. He shot me an unexpected question. "Watson, I presume sun-up would have had a vital role in your Regiment's confrontation with Ayub Khan at the Battle of Maiwand. Isn't that where you received an arrow in your right leg?"

"Left shoulder," I replied. "And it was a Jezail long-arm rifle bullet, not an arrow."

"My point is, Watson, did you become something of an expert on the daily motion of the sun?"

"I had to, yes," I responded.

"To the point you can calculate the very moment of sunrise?"

"Yes, Holmes, but it's far from as simple as you might think. First, you must decide upon your definition of sunrise – is it when the middle of the sun crosses the horizon, or the top edge, or the bottom edge? Also, do you take the horizon to be sea level, or do you take into account the topography? In addition, what of the Earth's atmosphere? It can bend the light so that the sun appears to rise a few moments earlier or later than if there were no atmosphere."

Holmes's expression turned from one of interest to impatience. He tore the briar from his mouth. "Yes, Watson, yes," he flared. "I consider a man's brain is like an empty attic. We must stock it with just such furniture as we choose. I merely want to know whether – given a while with a note-book and pencil – you can calculate the exact time this photograph was taken?"

I replied, "If we say sunrise refers to the time the middle of the disc of the sun appears on the horizon, considered unobstructed relative to the location of interest, and assuming atmospheric conditions to be average, and being sure to include the sun's declination from the time of the year…"

"Yes, yes, *yes!*" Holmes bellowed. "Take all of that into account, by all means! And let me know when you've made the calculation."

A telephone call from Holmes had ensured we were greeted at the Museum's imposing entrance by Sir Frederick Kenyon, the Director of the British Museum. Sir Frederick was a palaeographer and biblical and classical scholar of the Old School. Our host led us to a small antechamber. The first drawer he opened revealed a glittering array of gold hoops and gold rivets, several silver collars and neck-rings, a silver arm, a fragment of a Permian ring, and a silver penannular brooch. Each was meticulously labelled. Sir Frederick picked out a sword pommel. "Mediaeval battles were Lacey's life's work – the Battle of Fulford, the Siege of Exeter... Never have I had a colleague who worked with such application. For years at a time he would hardly leave to go home at night – that is, until..." He paused.

"Until?" I echoed.

Sir Frederick looked at Holmes. "I don't know how else to put it – until the occasion when Mr. Holmes failed to come to his help in finding the missing artefacts." A flush of colour sprang to Holmes's pale cheeks.

I interjected quickly, "Was it from this drawer the items Lacey described in his letter as being of no intrinsic value were disappearing?" The Director shook his head.

"No." He pulled open a second drawer. "From here."

The drawer was empty except for an envelope. It contained the letter I penned years earlier to the former Keeper of Antiquities, apologising for Holmes's refusal to become involved in the investigation. I had reconstructed Holmes's own words to read: *"Mr. Sherlock Holmes sends his regrets. He is attending to his bee-farm in the South Downs and will not be taking cases for the foreseeable future."*

"The missing artefacts were in this drawer," Sir Frederick continued. "Here's where Lacey kept the more common or garden pieces found at various battle-sites. Broken sword-blades and the like. Miscellany too lacking in value or utility even for the local peasantry to pick up. Nevertheless he took the theft very hard." Sir Frederick looked at my companion. "Mr. Holmes, I understood your refusal to waste your time on what must have seemed such a trivial matter. There wasn't a gold or silver item or precious jewel among the lot. Despite this, Lacey did seem unusually affected by Dr. Watson's letter. He grew secretive. Now I reflect on it, it was as though he was developing a clandestine plan."

Sir Frederick continued, "I noticed another change in his behaviour too. Other people's fame began to obsess him. He claimed his own name would become as famous in the annals of Archaeology as Mr. Charles Dawson's in Anthropology after Dawson pronounced the human-like skull he had uncovered near Piltdown to be the 'missing link' between ape and man."

I asked, "Did you have any idea what Lacey meant?"

The Museum Director shrugged. "One day I came in upon him unexpectedly. He was bent over that table studying a drawing. He said it involved electrical theory, but elaborated no further."

"Electrical theory?" Holmes repeated, followed by "Do you recall anything from the drawing itself?"

The Director shook his head. "I chanced only a quick glance before Lacey slipped the sketch under some other papers. There were wires. I spotted a few words in French. I remember there were two large wheels, one at each end of the legs of a bipod. Oh yes, something about the wheels was odd. They weren't upright like a dog-cart or other means of conveyance. They were flat on the ground. My curiosity overcame me. "Lacey," I said, "I'd be grateful if you kindly let me in on this secret of yours!" He muttered something about unexploded bombs. Then he got up from the table and said he'd been meaning to talk to me about retirement. He said if Europe's greatest Consulting Detective couldn't be bothered to look into the theft of artefacts from the British Museum, his faith in human beings was gone. A month or so later, he handed in his resignation and quit."

"What were the words in French?" I asked.

"'*Faisceau hertzien*'," came the reply. "I'm told that means *wireless beam.*

The great doors of the Museum shut behind us. I hailed a motorised hackney. "Waste of time coming all the way here, wasn't it, Holmes!" I remarked, "I can't say we learnt much about anything."

Holmes's eyebrows arched. "To the contrary, Watson, I think we learned a very great deal. Take Lacey's violent reaction when he received your letter. He even handed in his resignation! I'd have expected him to be exercised if the priceless gold and jewelled artefacts had been filched but not over a few worthless trinkets."

Holmes continued, "Don't you think it odd none of the valuable items went missing, despite being right next to the drawer containing ordinary relics of no intrinsic value. You'd have thought even the most common or garden sneak thief in something of a hurry can spot the difference between a gold torque and a rusty link from a dead Saxon's chain-mail armour."

In response to my wave a cab halted at the kerb in front of us. Once seated, Holmes mused. "Why would the loss of a few worthless battlefield gew-gaws generate such a clamour from the Keeper?"

"Monomania perhaps?" I answered. "As you know, there's a term the French novelist Honore de Balzac invented, '*idée fixe*', describing how an obsession may be accompanied by complete sanity in every other way."

Holmes asked, "What do you make of the other curious matter, the machine depicted in the blueprint? A bipod with two large wheels flat against the ground?"

"I haven't the faintest idea, Holmes, nor why the subject of unexploded bombs would come up at the British Museum."

"True," Holmes responded thoughtfully. "Explosives are an odd subject for a Keeper of Antiquities."

We reached Victoria Station. The train trundled across the bridge over the Thames. We were on our way back to Sussex.

After a lengthy walk in Holmes's woods and fields we returned to the farmhouse. I struck a match on my boot and put it to the fire laid earlier by Mrs. Keppler to ward off the country damp. The ancient hearth blazed up as heartily as in our days at 221b, Baker Street, but rather than the sea-coal in our London fireplace the flames here on the Downs were fuelled from the abundant local oak, known as the Weed of

Sussex. I opened my note-book and said, "Holmes, you asked where the sun was at the instant the camera shutter was released. Judging by the shadows in the photograph, I believe the photograph was taken when the geometric centre of the rising sun was eighteen degrees below low hills to the southeast. Around 6:40 a.m. was the first moment there would have been enough light."

My companion absorbed this in silence. A few minutes later he asked in a sympathetic tone, "If Captain Watson of the Army Medical Department were to consult Dr. John H. Watson M.D., at the latter's renowned medical practice in Marylebone, would Dr. Watson tell the Captain he has fully recovered from a frightful ordeal in Mesopotamia, followed by incarceration in a Turkish dungeon?"

"Thank you, Holmes," I replied, touched and surprised by this rare concern. "You may take it the Captain's heart would be certified as strong as that of the proverbial ox. Daily walks on the warship returning Captain Watson to these shores, combined with the fine food of the Naval Officer's Mess, completely restored him."

"Excellent!" my companion exclaimed. He leaned with his back against the shutters, the deep-set grey eyes narrowing, and adding enigmatically, "Watson, we hold in our hand the threads of one of the strangest cases ever to perplex a man's brain, yet we lack the one or two clues which are needful to complete a theory of mine. Ah, I see you yawning. I suggest you retire. I shall tarry over a pipe a while longer to see if light can be cast on our path ahead."

The country air and the warmth of the log-fire had indeed taken their effect. I hadn't the slightest idea what Holmes was up to or whether or how the strength of Captain Watson's heart could have anything to do with the present perplexing case. I fell into a comfortable bed and a restful sleep.

I was dreaming of I know not what when a loud rat-tat-tat came on my bedroom door. "Watson!" Holmes called out.

"We must throw our brains into action. Dress quickly!" I opened an eye. Through the window, Venus and Mars were in close conjunction, bright in an otherwise cloudy night sky. "What is it, Holmes?" I returned indignantly. "Can't it wait till dawn?"

The door flew open. My impatient host entered, dressed for the outdoors in Norfolk jacket and knickerbockers, with a cloth cap upon his head. "Watson, the *genius loci*. As you know, I'm a believer in visiting the scene of the crime. It is essential in the proper exercise of deduction to take the perspective of those involved. I have just returned from Battle. I must return there with you straight away. Just one thread remains, my dear fellow. You are the one person who can provide it."

An hour later Holmes and I stood side by side on the spot where William the Conqueror's knights crushed King Harold's housecarls and his Saxon freemen. Holmes flapped a hand over a patch of grass. "I estimate Lacey's body lay here. Watson. How long before the geometric centre of the rising sun reaches eighteen degrees below the horizon?"

I looked to the south-east. "Not more than five minutes," I replied, adding, "May I say I'm at a complete loss to know what in heaven's name we're doing here, Holmes. The dawn hasn't even..."

"Then Watson, you must have your answer!" Holmes shouted. "Turn to face the Abbey!"

I whirled around. A terrifying apparition burst upon my startled gaze. With no sound audible above my stentorian breathing, a knight in chain-mail astride a huge charger was flying silently down the slope towards me, a boar image on his helmet, on an arm a kite shield limned with a Crusader cross and six *Fleur De Lis*. Half-a-dozen cowled monks rose out of the ground behind him, menacing, crouching, uttering strange cries. I broke into a cold, clammy sweat. My muscles twitched uncontrollably. I felt I was about to crash to the ground. The immense horse and rider passed by in a second, dashing on until the pair merged with the spectral mist rising from a clump of bushes a hundred yards down the slope. I turned to face the ghostly monks. There was no-one there. It was as though a preternatural visitation had returned to the Netherworld with the first shafts of the rising sun.

I dropped to all fours, dazed. Holmes's voice came to me faintly, as though from a distant shore: "Watson, my dear fellow, are you all right? You've had a terrible shock." The familiar voice brought me back to sanity. I was still shaking with fright.

In the same reassuring tone, Holmes went on, "The phantoms have gone, my dear friend. They've returned to their rest. They will not be back until the next anniversary of the Battle of Hastings."

The terror I endured for those few seconds was dissipating. I looked around the empty sward. "Where on Earth...?" I began.

"Tunnels, my dear fellow," Holmes answered. "Monks and other ecclesiasticals. Landed Gentry. Knights Templar. Abbots. All particularly given to tunnels."

Holmes looked at me closely. "Again I ask, are you all right, my dear fellow?"

"I am nearly recovered," I said. "I appreciate your evident concern, Holmes, but you are clearly not an innocent party to this strange event. I deserve and demand an explanation."

Holmes seated himself on the ground at my side. "Two clues put me on a scent, Watson. First, the trace evidence around us here." His finger described an ellipse following the trajectory of the ghostly horse as it galloped down to the swamp. "Look there, and there," he ordered.

I stared at the series of depressions in the grass. "But Holmes," I protested, "while those indentations may fit where a horse's hooves would have landed, they are both too shallow and too square for the marks of a horse ridden at speed!"

"My dear Captain Watson, I take it despite your service in the Far East you failed to hear of mediaeval Japanese straw horse-sandals known as *umugatsu*? They were tied between the fetlock and hoof to give traction on wet terrain and to muffle the sound of the hooves, and to deceive by eliminating the deep cuts hooves would inflict on damp earth. I think we can credit the local schoolmaster for his scholarship."

"Nice touch. The Crusader shield too," I remarked sarcastically, "when you consider the first Crusade didn't commence until thirty years after the Battle of Hastings."

I fingered my pulse. It was returning to normal. "And the second of two clues, Holmes?"

"The second lay in the difference between the print I purchased and the same photograph as it appeared in *The Battle Observer*. The editor wanted only the corpse's face and the arrow, therefore, Hanson enlarged the middle of the print. This brought out a granulated effect in the grass under the head. But why? Why was there any graininess about the background at all? Why weren't the blades of grass as much in focus as the face and arrow?"

"Holmes," I responded, "I have given that question some thought. Forgive me if what I'm about to propose sounds absurd, but I'm very far from being unacquainted with cameras, as you know. The only explanation is the camera must have been positioned much higher up than if held by someone standing on the ground in the normal way. Getting the face in precise focus at the greater distance would mean anything deeper would be less in focus but this effect would show up only when the photograph was enlarged."

"The very conclusion I came to myself, Watson!" my companion exclaimed, rubbing his hands in delight. The *occipitofrontalis* muscles of my forehead wrinkled. I asked, "But why would Hanson stretch his arms high over his head to take the photo?"

"He wouldn't," came the response. "He didn't need to. He was seated on a horse. The knight was none other than *The Observer* photographer himself."

I waved at the field stretching away above us. "Holmes, how in Heaven's name did you get them to cooperate?"

"Not eight hours ago, I paid Hanson a visit," Holmes replied. "He admitted everything. I told him he and his co-conspirators could be in mortal danger, accused of murder, and that my silence was not safeguard enough – others may yet make the same deduction. He said 'I'm the one who thought up the caper. If anyone is to meet the hangman, it should be me. I just wanted to scare Lacey off. I never intended anyone to die.' I told him I had something in mind. He and the monks were to reassemble here before dawn today." Holmes tapped his watch and raised and dropped an arm. "At my signal, the knight was to charge straight at the man in a captain's uniform at my side. The monks were once again to spring up like dragon's teeth, yelling any doggerel they could remember from schoolboy Latin."

The explanation jolted me to the core. "Holmes!" I yelled. I broke off, breathing hard. "Holmes," I repeated, "I once described you as a brain without a heart, as deficient in human sympathy as you are pre-eminent in intelligence. Are you proving me right? Are you saying that despite Lacey's frightful death, you deliberately exposed me to an identical fate?"

"Yes, my dear Captain," Holmes broke in, chuckling, "I did. You must remember I took the precaution of checking on your health with a Dr. Watson famed on two Continents for his medical skills. He pronounced your heart strong as an ox. Who am I to dispute his diagnosis?"

"And if the good Dr. Watson had made a misjudgement?" I asked ruefully.

"High stakes indeed, Watson," came the rejoinder. "I would have lost a great friend, and a hapless crew of locals their best witness, leaving me bereft and them open to a further charge of murder!"

My legs still felt shaky. "Holmes," I begged, "why are you so adamantly on these people's side?"

"Think of this small town, Watson," he replied. "Eight hundred and fifty years ago, when Duke William crossed the Channel, there was no human settlement here, just a quiet stretch of rough grazing. Look at it now! Without the battlefield, it would be nothing, a backwater, a small and isolated market-town. Imagine Royal Windsor without the Castle, Canterbury without the Cathedral. Visitors to this battleground provide the underpinning of every merchant on the High Street, the hoteliers and publicans, even *The Battle Observer* itself, dependent on advertising Philpott's Annual Summer Sales and the like. The mock monks and a spectral knight on horseback can fairly be accused of one thing – trying to protect their livelihoods. Napoleon greatly incensed the English by calling us 'a nation of shopkeepers'. He was right. If visitors stop coming, the hotels die. The souvenir shops die. The cafés and restaurants close. Lacey and his new technology threatened all that."

Holmes pointed to where ghostly horse and rider had disappeared. "Have you recovered enough to walk down to that clump of bushes? I anticipate we shall find something there of extreme interest."

At the bottom of the slope, a small bridge took us to a patch of marshland dotted about with bushes and reeds into which horse and rider had disappeared. Holmes's former quick pace slowed like the Clouded Leopard searching out its prey. With a grunt of satisfaction, he darted forward, calling out "Come, Watson – give me a hand!" A pair of wooden spars jutted from the mud. A spade half-floated on the mud a few feet beyond. We dragged the contraption to a patch of dry ground. It was the physical embodiment of the blueprint the Keeper of Antiquities had tried to hide at the British Museum.

Held upright, the bipod was perhaps three feet in height. It was exactly as described by Sir Frederick: The two wheels were not wheels of a small cart, but circles of wood and metal lying flush with the ground, some twenty-four inches apart. A set of wires led to a half-submerged metal box filled with vacuum tubes and a heavy battery.

I pointed. "Holmes, those are Audion vacuum tubes. I've seen them used in wireless technology. This must be the secret invention Lacey hinted at."

"If he had not built it, Watson, he might still be alive." Holmes continued, "I pondered long and hard about '*Faisceau hertzien*', and the reference to unexploded bombs. Then by chance my brother Mycroft called to say he had been seconded to the War Office for the duration. In the greatest confidence, he told me the French 6th Engineer Regiment at Verdun-sur-Meuse has been developing a machine using wireless beams to detect German mines. Somehow Lacey must have heard about it. He realised at once he could adapt it to search for metal artefacts at ancient battlegrounds."

He pointed at the spade. "He criss-crossed these fields at night using a device which could spot even a silver penny dropped nine centuries ago. With it, he would be able to detect every metal artefact left by Duke William's and King Harold's men. He planned to remove anything traceable to 1066 and add it to the artefacts he buried in a field of his choosing some miles away. In an act of great evil against the noble profession of Archaeology, at a moment of maximum publicity, he would claim to be the person who had discovered the real field where the Battle of Hastings was fought. Lacey's spurious location for the battle would be several miles away. He didn't give a jot to the fact the town's prosperity would come to an abrupt end. The location would be quite disconnected to the town. Even *The Observer* would go out of business. As it happens, one recent moonlit night Brian Hanson saw this phantom-like figure moving slowly across the landscape. He recognised

Lacey. He spied on him for a while and guessed what he was up to. The townsfolk had to work fast."

"Should we report our findings to the local police, Holmes?" I asked.

"By no means," came the firm reply.

I turned to stare at my companion. "But...but surely, now we know..."

"Watson, we need do nothing but wait to see if the matter progresses or simply dies away. If the latter, a kindly fate has taken its course. If the former, thanks to you no jury of twelve good men and true will convict for murder."

"How can that be, Holmes?" I asked, "when indisputably their actions caused the death of a man. How can they escape the hangman's noose?"

"Because of 'intent', Watson," Holmes began. "Our motley crew of locals didn't have murder in mind. They rose up out of the ground dressed as the disquieted souls of long-dead Benedictines and inadvertently caused Lacey's heart to give way. Their plan was to frighten him off and fling his infernal contrivance and spade into the swamp. That *that* was their intent is the more credible, thanks to your survival. They now have a good case to plead *Mens rea* – no mental intent to kill. At worst manslaughter, not murder."

"The arrow?" I asked.

"Admittedly a barbarous act," Holmes replied, "but the man was already dead. Hanson hoped to confuse the coroner, to make him conclude the arrow caused the stricken expression on the corpse's face. Otherwise, alarm bells would ring, and a case of murder arise."

Now mollified, I asked rhetorically, "You mean, who would want to associate the vile crime of murder with these dear old homesteads set in a smiling and beautiful countryside? Another case resolved, Holmes. Let us leave the good people of Battle to their commemorative preparations and repair to our favourite eatery deep among the Downs – in short, visit the Tiger Inn and partake of a hearty lunch."

We heaved the spade deeper into the marsh and marked the unexploded-bomb-detector's location for retrieval by Mycroft Holmes's agents at a later time. As we walked back across the small bridge I said, "There's a matter you have not explained. Why did the Keeper of Antiquities react in such a choleric way to your refusal to investigate?"

"It was a most devious ploy quite worthy of arch-criminal Moriarty of old, Watson. A snub was precisely what Lacey wanted. I should have smelt a rat by the way he worded his request – *'I shall of course understand if this case is of little interest to you, Mr. Holmes, the missing articles being of no intrinsic value whatsoever'*. That's hardly as compelling as *'Mr. Holmes, while the relics are of scant intrinsic value, from the historical point of view they are very nearly unique'*. Your letter informing him of my refusal came like Manna from Heaven. He could show Sir Frederick he'd tried to bring in a most famous Consulting Detective. No-one would ever dream the larcenist was Lacey himself. He could then use the pilfered artefacts to 'salt' the field of his choosing."

"Thereby," I added, "fulfilling his ambition to become as famous in the archaeological world as Dawson in the world of the palaeontologist and anatomist."

Together we walked across the historic fields. A line of horse-drawn cabs was forming at the Abbey entrance, the fine arrangement of bays and cobs snorting into their nose-bags, ready for the day's influx of visitors. We went to a Landau driven by a pair.

"Cabbie, the Tiger Inn," Holmes instructed. "An extra guinea for you from the Captain here if we arrive before their kitchen runs out of that well-armed sea creature, the lobster."

The End

1 – The case was published under the title *Sherlock Holmes and the Sword of Osman* MX Publishing.

The Pegasus Affair

by Tim Symonds

In which Holmes and Watson encounter
an acquaintance from 'Shoscombe Old Place'

I awoke early. The rays of an early morning spring sun splayed across the room from the Adam style marginal wall mirror. Despite the advent of middle years and a dodgy leg from fighting Ayub Khan at the Battle of Maiwand, I leapt from the bed. My first electric vehicle would be delivered that morning, a 1916 automobile purchased direct from the factory, the Belmont Electric Auto Company of Wyandotte, Michigan.

The Belmont was advertised as noiseless, clean, durable, comfortable, simple in operation and, compared to the noxious internal combustion engine, odourless. She had cost more than 1,600 American dollars, delivered to my door. The price included Goodyear long-distance electric tyres and a handsome set of goggles and gauntlet gloves. The pale yellow leather matching the paint-work was decided after a thorough perusal of sketches, watercolours, leather and fabric samples, and paint chips.

Two hours later I was in possession of the gleaming four-seater limousine. "She's silent, all right," the delivery chauffeur replied, handing me the goggles and gloves. "The start is dependable and immediate, but take care with the controls. They're a bit jerky." We chatted about the Belmont's elliptic rear springs until a hansom cab came by to whisk the helpful fellow away with a generous gratuity in his pocket.

I returned to my surgery via the Tradesman's Entrance. An envelope lay on the hall table. I returned to it after putting the motor-car documents into the safe. It contained a newspaper cutting from *The Eastbourne Chronicle*, but no accompanying letter. It must be from Sherlock Holmes, I

107

decided. He was living in retirement on the Sussex Downs, not far from Eastbourne. The article was headed: *'Grand National Horse Race To Be Run For The First Time Away From Aintree'*, followed by,

> *The Stewards at the Gatwick Racecourse have asked* The Chronicle *to remind readers that preparations are now complete for the Grand National Handicap Steeplechase to take place this Friday, March 24th. A special course has been constructed at Gatwick due to the fact Aintree, the home of the Grand National, has been commandeered by the Army for the duration of the War against Germany. To avoid confusion, the race this year will be called 'The Racecourse Association Steeplechase'.*

> *The course will be precisely the same distance as at Aintree, four miles and eight-hundred-fifty-six yards over two laps. Twenty-nine fences have been constructed under the supervision of five leading jumps trainers, though without the challenge of Beecher's Brook with its four-foot ten-inch fence and five-foot six-inch brook. The prize money is expected to be high with the winner receiving five hundred gold sovereigns.*

The cutting brought a smile to my lips. For years Holmes had engaged in banter over my betting habit, even accusing me of getting myself badly wounded at the Battle of Maiwand in Afghanistan merely to get the Army pension of eleven shillings and sixpence a day to throw on the horses – yet here he was reminding me, albeit unnecessarily, of the greatest steeple-chase of the betting calendar. I looked up at the clock. Mid-day. With my wife away, I decided to hand over the afternoon patients to a *locum* and drive down to show off my new steed to Holmes at his isolated bee-farm. The rolling chalk downland and steep undulations would give a good sense of what an electrical vehicle could manage. We might celebrate the arrival of the Belmont by dining at The Tiger Inn, a favourite haunt whenever I spent a day or two as Holmes's guest. I sent a telegram telling my old friend to expect me that evening and went up to the attic to retrieve my tailored hacking jacket and checked cravat from a box of summer wear.

I entered the familiar landscape of the South Downs in silence except for the swishing of the car tyres. All around were the early throes of spring. Hazel and willow catkins fidgeted in the hedgerows, the leaf litter speckled with the white stars of wood anemone and wild yellow primroses and celandine. Holmes's farmhouse came into sight. As usual he was waiting for me in the yard, telegram in hand. "And the name of your young mistress?" he asked, nodding at the Belmont.

I had anticipated the question. "Empress," I replied.

An eyebrow went up. "After the winner of the 1880 Grand National, I presume? How sentimental. If I remember rightly, that was the year before we took lodgings together at 221B, Baker Street."

"It was," I agreed, "but of the two events, the most memorable was the five guineas I wagered on the filly."

Holmes's next question took me by surprise. "To what do I owe the pleasure of your company on a Thursday? I would expect you on a weekend. Have you abandoned your patients today solely for the delights of the English countryside?"

I replied, "Surely you remember! Tomorrow's the Grand National at the Gatwick Races! You sent me the newspaper cutting."

My host's brow wrinkled. "Cutting, Watson?" came the rejoinder.

I tugged it from a pocket. He read it intently, returning it with, "So I did! Now come inside. My housekeeper will bring us tea. You can tell me all about your new mechanical filly. They say electric cars will be the death of thousands. No-one can hear them coming."

We stepped on to the verandah. "Holmes," I said, "I hope you'll be my guest at the races tomorrow. Empress will get us there in no time at all."

Holmes waved me on towards the comfortable sitting room, giving an apologetic shake of his head. "I think not, my dear friend. April approaches. I have duties toward my bees. The queens have to start laying eggs."

I protested, "Bees have been around from before the Age of the Dinosaurs. They managed perfectly well without S. Holmes Esq. at their beck and call."

"My worker bees are as much as six months old," Holmes replied. "In bee terms, they are geriatric. They can't hold out much longer. Stimulated by the workers, the queens can lay fifteen hundred eggs a day – more than their own body weight. They require a daily dose of syrup until the blackthorn comes into proper bloom. If there's anything going on at the Gatwick Races after that, I'll be happy to join you. As for tomorrow, I do have to be away for a while in the afternoon. I'd take it as a particular favour if you'll stay and administer the syrup in my stead."

I stared at him incredulously. "Holmes, under almost every other circumstance I would meet your request in an instant, but to give up the chance to be at the Grand National just to feed your little blighters? Absolutely not!"

The journey to Gatwick was uneventful. In no great hurry, I stopped to lunch at a small pub at Ditchling Common. I arrived at the Racecourse amid a welter of Model T Tourers and elegant Victorias, and parked the Belmont next to a monster American LaFrance 14-Litre Roadster. There was an hour to go before the start of the Grand National. Ticket in hand, I pushed through the excited crowd to the Enclosure. Just ahead, a man approaching middle-age caught my attention. He was tall, clean-shaven, with a firm, austere expression. Our eyes met. He seemed to turn away sharply yet there was something familiar about him. Then I realised.

"Good Lord!" I burst out aloud, delighted to have come across him once more. Unless I was completely misled by the passage of time – nearly fourteen years – it was John Mason, Head Trainer at the Shoscombe Stables. Alarmed by the strange antics of his employer, Sir Robert Norberton, Mason had called upon Holmes at our Baker Street lodgings. My old comrade-in-arms solved the case with the help of a spaniel. I planned to publish the bizarre affair someday in *The Strand Magazine* under the title 'The Adventure of Shoscombe Old Place'.

There were one or two post-mortem points I could clear up with Mason right now. I came up behind him and tapped him on the shoulder. He turned swiftly. A long, hard stare was followed by a brusque, "And what do you want, sir? I have all the tips on winners I need!"

I broke into a friendly guffaw, taking the rebuff as an effort to be amusing, after which we would shake hands in convivial greeting, but I was wrong. The look remained savage. No handshake was forthcoming. "Mason," I repeated, "you remember me! Dr. Watson. Back in '02. Sherlock Holmes and I came to Berkshire in the matter of Sir Robert Norberton's peculiar behaviour."

Mason's voice got louder. "There may be dozens of Dr. Watsons, for all I know," he retorted, "but I hope you're not purporting to be the *real* Dr. John Watson..." His right hand rose as though to give me a hard push for my insolence, "...*or are you so purporting?*"

I exclaimed, "I repeat, Holmes and I came to your stables to solve a strange little mystery concerning your employer. If you are John Mason, the Head Trainer at the Shoscombe Stud, it's inconceivable that you don't recognise me."

The man's response grew more heated. "Inconceivable that I see right through your music hall performance? But it's a fact! I have no doubt the *real* Dr. Watson has a thousand personators, all pretending they're comrades of Sherlock Holmes, all no doubt trying to borrow money. For a start, the Watson I met in Berkshire wore a fine military moustache like a Cossack, not that ridiculous little 'tache you sport on your upper lip. You clearly have practiced your deceit – the skimmer on your head is very like Dr. Watson's, finished with a smart black Petersham ribbon, but a gentleman of his standing would never wear a straw boater so early in the season. What's more, I observed you hurrying to catch me. You limp on your left leg, whereas I'm certain it was the real Dr. Watson's right leg which was struck by a jezail bullet at the Battle of Maiwand." Gesticulating angrily, he continued, "I deem you to be an imposter. Remove yourself from my presence, and at once, or I warn you, I shall have you arrested! I am well known at the Gatwick Races. If you dare accost me further, I shall not hesitate to call on the stewards to have you thrown out. Do you understand?" At this he turned on his heel.

My flabbergasted gaze followed the tall figure until he melted into a gaggle of sniggering spectators. The unpleasant encounter puzzled and badly unsettled me. How dare the fellow suggest my moustache had ever been like a Cossack's, of such ridiculous length they had to tuck them behind their ears. I walked to the enclosure and tried to bring my attention to bear on the race card. I had a long-standing preference for odds of 11-to-4. There was a horse at those odds by the name of Cinzano, entered by Sir Robert, Mason's employer. The presence of the horse explained Mason's attendance, but not his vile attitude.

I turned my field glasses on the throng of spectators in the stand. Scattered among society women in over-sized hats stacked with plumes of feathers, bows, flowers, birds, lace, and tulle would be horse-racing aficionados known to me from Aintree and other great racecourses, in which case I would join them. Through the glasses, I noticed a rough-looking cove pushing his way through the crowd. He was clad in seafaring garb, with an old pea-jacket buttoned up to a coloured scarf around his throat. Years of dried sweat had left dark patches under the arm-pits.

The face was badly pocked, perhaps smallpox contracted in some Asian port. He stopped here and there to sell a rolled-up piece of paper. I wondered which vicissitudes had brought him to an impoverished living peddling fanciful tips to the gullible at the Gatwick Races. Had he spent rum-soaked years in the Merchant Marine, sailing from Takoradi on the Gold Coast to the mangrove swamps of Tanjung Benoa?

Just when I feared the man was about to accost me with his little slips of paper, he came to a halt some five or six feet away. I checked my money was safe in a buttoned-up inside pocket and braced myself to refuse an offer of a 'dead cert winner' in exchange for a shilling when, with a West Country accent, the stranger spoke, as though to some invisible being in front of him: "That's a fine straw hat you're wearing, sir, and worn at a becomingly rakish angle."

"Now look here," I began, still seething from my encounter with John Mason.

I was about to follow with "I've had enough impertinence for one day" when the man interrupted *sotto voce*: "Quite the gathering of the clans, eh, Watson? I see you encountered Major Mason – no, look elsewhere, please. He saved your life just now, you know."

"Holmes!" I declared, quickly averting my gaze. "What on Earth are you doing here? And what do you mean *Major* Mason? And what do you mean he saved my life? He was downright rude, if you mean *that* saved my life!"

"I mean precisely that," came the reply. "You were in great danger. I'll explain about the military rank later. I wasn't the one who sent you that newspaper cutting. The sender was extraordinarily keen to remind you about the Grand National, wasn't he! But why anonymously? I surmised he knew of my arrangement to meet Mason here, in disguise. Whoever sent it wanted to be sure you'd be here, too."

"And why would he want that?" I asked.

"So you would lead him to me," came the reply. "Shooting Dr. Watson on a racecourse on Grand National Day would be a quixotic end for you, but the plotter knew I would come running to see if your life could be saved, exposing me to an equally deadly shot, no matter what my disguise. Murderous cunning of that order is in the compass of only one old enemy of ours still living, namely – "

"Colonel Sebastian Moran," I stuttered.

"None other," Holmes replied. "If Mason had greeted you as the *real* John Watson, right now you would be at St. Peter's Gate, trying to talk your way into Heaven."

I said, my heart pounding, "What makes you think Moran wouldn't know my face perfectly well?"

"Because to the best of my knowledge at no time has he ever had a good look at you. When I engineered his capture in Camden House it was by torch-light and at that time Inspector Lestrade and I were the chief targets of his fury." Holmes gave a slight motion of his hand towards a clump of *Cupressus sempervirens* some two-hundred yards away. "Even though he had you in his sights, he needed to be sure you were the real Dr. Watson, the proof Mason would provide if he returned your enthusiastic greeting."

Moran's credentials with a rifle were unparalleled. Only with great restraint was I able to avoid turning my field glasses on the copse of Italian cypresses indicated by Holmes. It was deeply unnerving to know the Chief of Staff to the erstwhile Napoleon of Crime, Professor Moriarty, was so near. Moran, formerly of the 1st Bangalore Pioneers, served in the Jowaki Expedition of 1877-1878, and in the Second Anglo-Afghan War, for which he was mentioned in despatches. He may even have come dressed as he was when we saw him last, opera-hat pushed to the back of his head, an evening dress shirt-front peeking out through the open overcoat.

Although older than me by twelve years, he would still possess the thin, projecting nose, the bald forehead by now rather higher, though the huge grizzled moustache may have disappeared. Given a choice, I would prefer another encounter with Ayub Khan's fanatical warriors at a second Battle of Maiwand than with the old *shikaree*.

In a low voice I said, "Moran has long since been on the loose. What makes you so sure our old enemy is here?"

"I recognised his sentinel while scouring around," Holmes replied. "A garrotter by trade, and a remarkable performer upon the Jew's harp. As to Major Mason, he can explain his rank and the real reason he's at the Gatwick Races."

"Real reason?" I queried. "Surely it's because Sir Robert has a horse in a race?"

"It's to do with a horse, yes," came the enigmatic reply, "but not one you would bet your Army pension on. While you have your field-glasses, swing them to the south-east. See the control tower of a small airfield? We must get there straight away. Mason is waiting there for us."

Forgetting the covert nature of our conversation, I exploded, "Really, Holmes! Have you gone completely frothy? I've come all this way to see the Grand National. It takes place in twenty minutes. Here I stay until the race is over." I dropped my voice to a whisper. "The *Grand National*, Holmes!" I repeated. "Which horse are you tipping on those little rolls of paper?"

"Vermouth," came the reply. "Ridden by Jack Reardon. A shilling from you later, if you please."

On my way to the line of bookies I glanced back. The old salt had disappeared. I took his advice and placed a substantial bet on Vermouth.

Another thrilling Grand National was over. One horse fell and eight pulled up. Vermouth was the winner at *100/8*. As soon as I collected my winnings, I walked back to Empress and drove into the tiny airfield through a side-gate. The sentry checked my name, saluted, and pointed me towards Mason. Holmes at his side was still in his Ancient Mariner disguise, the facial pock-marking intact. Mason had changed into a military uniform. He seized my hand in clear pleasure.

"Good to see you again, Dr. Watson," he exclaimed. He gestured towards the distant enclosure. "By now you'll have understood my odd behaviour. At any moment I was expecting the crack of a tiger rifle. Let's jump into your wonderful limousine and drive to a certain spot out of sight and earshot of the world."

Holmes withdrew a telegram from his pocket. "First, though, take a look at this." It was headed '*Royal Navy Air Station Eastchurch. Top Secret*', followed by '*The Vickers F.B.5 gunship, Serial No. 1535, was removed from its hangar last night by a man using forged authorisation and matching the description you sent. As agreed, we made no effort to intercept or report the aircraft missing.*' I handed the telegram back with a quizzical look.

"Take a glance over my shoulder," Mason ordered. "What do you see?"

Standing all by itself at the far end of the runway was a two-seat pusher military biplane. "A Vickers F.B.5?" I hazarded.

"Right first time," Mason replied. "No. 1535. Landed here early this morning, pretending it had engine trouble. The trap is set."

Empress took us deep into narrow country lanes before John Mason began his explanation. "Dr. Watson, I should start with, '*Once upon a time . . .*' and it did all start some time ago, not long after I invited you and Mr. Holmes to Shoscombe Stables, that time when Sir Robert was acting so strangely. The fact he was threatened with immediate bankruptcy over his debts had a lot to do with it. He was saved when Shoscombe Prince came first in the Derby.

"The win paid off all creditors with enough left over to re-establish the stud and retain me as Head Trainer. Soon, the stables were home to eight first-class stallions. A subsequent winter proved to be particularly severe in the Vale of the White Horse. A blizzard began on Christmas Eve. The snow continued falling until New Year's Day. We couldn't risk exercising the horses in the appalling weather conditions yet it was essential to keep our riders fit. I remembered something Sir Robert had mentioned about the South African War. Our Army had a bad time with the Boer commandos because most of our riders weren't fit enough to take 'em on in the Veldt. He predicted we would have the same problem next time. The quickest way for England to train up riders wouldn't be by finding enough real horses and having horse and rider running wild over hill and dale. "We should invent a mechanical horse, a simulator, right at Shoscombe Old Place, Sir Robert opined", Mason continued. "Nothing came of the idea at the time. I forgot all about it until three or four years ago when war-fever started up. We heard that the Ottomans, with tens of thousands of cavalry, might join the Boche against us – Middle Eastern Theatre especially. I began to tinker in one of the stables. The aim was to come up with something a novice could straddle, a device which exactly mimicked the way real horses move, from flatwork to jumping, to fast work. And that's how it started."

"And your progress?" I asked.

"For public consumption, Dr. Watson, we must say wonderfully well, wonderfully well!"

Then Mason shook his head. "However, things didn't work out at Shoscombe. A mechanical horse is a fiendishly complicated thing. Sir Robert was about to give up when the Master of the Old Berkshire Hunt brought a mare to the stud for covering. Turns out, he's a Commissary-General in the

Army Service Corps Transport Department. I told him half in jest about *Project Pegasus*. He took it to heart. Things began to move fast.

"The War Office charged me with developing a fully-fledged simulator. I formed a brand new unit known as the 117 Motor Transport Company." His hand rose to touch the King's Imperial Crowns on his shoulder epaulettes. "I was given the rank of Major. From then on, work had to take place in the most exceptional secrecy. First I was ordered to put it about that *Project Pegasus* had failed, that we'd abandoned the idea completely."

I said, "But I don't understand. What has any of this to do with the Gatwick Races?"

"Shoscombe is set in wide-open countryside," Holmes interrupted. "The project needed to move, but it had to be where any sort of horse talk would hardly be noticed." He gestured back towards the control tower. "They moved here, with the added bonus of a dozen or so soldiers assigned to that little airfield in range of our present destination, but not so near as to attract attention from prying eyes."

As he spoke, we approached a large sign saying '*Halt! Go no further! Home Defence Corps – Mined Area.*'

"Carry on, Watson," Holmes said. "There aren't any mines around." He broke off to point at a small huddle of huts a mile or so distant. "Now turn onto these fields. See those old stables? The War Department requisitioned them from the Gatwick Race Course Company. You notice they're camouflaged. That's because the occasional Zeppelin comes over and pays the racecourse an unfriendly visit."

"We put our own stallions in most of the stables," said Mason, "but in one we built the mechanical horse. I've had regular supplies of oats and alfalfa dropped off outside each door, including the stable containing the simulator. After dark, one of my men comes back and distributes Pegasus's share of fodder among the other horses."

We bumped across open ground. "Perhaps you'll tell me how Colonel Sebastian Moran fits into all this?" I asked.

"That's where the plot thickens," Holmes responded. "What was it Hamlet said? - '*The play is the thing, wherein I'll catch the conscience of the king*'. A year or so ago, British counter-intelligence in Berlin reported overhearing a Commander - Fritz Prieger - expressing his intention to 'refresh' Germany's supply of spies in Britain. Prieger is head of sub-division N.I. of the *Nachrichten-Abteilung*, the German naval intelligence service. He spoke of recruiting 'a top agent', able to carry out even the most daring of projects. Outlines of the plan were tracked by British intelligence. Our main source was the Kaiser himself. He brought the subject up at several sessions of his War Cabinet and even boasted about it on a visit to Sultan Mehmed V in Constantinople. He told the Sultan that Prieger had made contact with someone who would be the spider at the centre of the web.

"This human arachnid would ruthlessly take whatever measure needed to get hold of a blueprint of any secret new weapon or, better still, get his hands on a working prototype. The man was described as well-known around London, someone of extreme guile, a meritorious past but murky present, and a habit of gambling at cards 'which leaves him with a constant thirst for money'.

"Moran," Holmes added. "And for '*money*' read '*gold*'."

Conversation was interrupted by our arrival at the line of huts. Mason jumped out, saying, "I'll run ahead to check everything's all right. Park the vehicle around the back, if you don't mind."

A minute later we heard a shout. Mason came rushing into the open. "He's gone!" he cried. "Pegasus has been stolen!"

"Watson!" I heard Holmes exclaim furiously, "you delayed us to watch the Grand National. That's when Moran must have taken his chance!" Horrified, I stared into the open stable. A rectangular compression in the pile of straw showed where the crate containing the dismantled mechanical horse had lain. The sound of a heavy aircraft engine starting up burst over the landscape. As one, we rushed outside.

The Vickers was taxiing down the runway. The engine roar increased. The pilot lifted the aircraft off the runway. "Quickly!" I called out. "Jump aboard! Empress can get us back there in less than twenty minutes. Major, you can order them to intercept the gunship and if necessary shoot it down."

"Good thinking!" Mason shouted. I rushed to the Belmont and engaged the starter only to find I was the only person in the vehicle. Turning, I saw Holmes and Mason bent over with laughter. The unseen pilot turned the Vickers, seeming deliberately to set a course right over us. Instantly my two companions ceased their expressions of amusement and began to jump up and down, shaking their fists at the aeroplane in impotent rage. A hand shot out from the cockpit and gave an insolent wave. Within seconds, the plane disappeared over the horizon, no doubt to turn on its final route well beyond our vision. I saw my two companions again begin laughing until their cheeks flushed.

I shouted, "I don't understand. How is this amusing? He'll soon be beyond interception."

"We can only hope so, Watson," Holmes gasped, before yet again he and Mason shook with renewed laughter.

The three of us settled on a grassy bank. "You see, Dr. Watson," Mason began, "I wasn't quite honest with you. Or better put, I was deliberately dishonest because Mr. Holmes and I knew we were under constant watch. Our counter-plot could fail on an instant. Up to a year ago everything had seemed on course. I had the 117 Motor Transport Company under my command. Any parts we needed, we could order from the Army Service Corps. Bit by bit, our mechanics slotted the pieces together. Six months ago, we were ready to try out Pegasus at a walk. The test at a canter would come next, mimicking a jump even later. Then the day came. A bevy of senior Light Cavalry officers invited themselves to the trials.

"We hit a serious snag. Pegasus wouldn't work with the weight of a brigadier on his back, even at a walk. He just shuddered and jerked. We ought to have designed separate mechanical horses, one set at a continuous trot, the other at a constant canter, not an all-in-one hybrid. I was in despair. I heard my mechanics talking among themselves in what seemed a consolatory manner. I asked what they were talking about. They refused to tell me. They said they could be cashiered for telling anyone, even an officer. I didn't take their 'no' for an answer. Now Mr. Holmes and I have something to show you." We walked to the far end of the stables, to what seemed to be a disused barrack room.

Mason swung open the heavy doors and waved me in. Instead of lines of uncomfortable Army cots and a stove, an immense rhomboid bulk loomed over us. It looked like a huge water tank, except it was sitting on tracks like an American caterpillar tractor.

"What on Earth is it?" I gasped.

Mason chuckled at my astonishment. "A landship. The mechanical engineers dub it 'the tank' – you'll guess why from its appearance. Unknown to me, my mechanics had been ordered to work on a top-secret parallel project to Pegasus. It's a modern siege engine designed to climb a five-foot earth parapet and cross up to an eight-foot gap."

Patting the behemoth he added, "These monsters can house a crew of ten, two machine guns, and a naval six-pounder gun. They're about to go into full production. Turns out, the officer in charge of the land ship project heard we were carrying out work here," Mason explained. "He deliberately located the prototype at the far end of the line of sheds. I hadn't the slightest inkling anything was going on hardly forty yards away, so complete was the blanket of secrecy."

Mason paused. "Glad as I was to hear about another secret weapon," he went on, "I still felt a sense of despair. Everything I'd been doing had proved a waste of time. By contrast, this landship passed its night trials with flying colours. But what if word of their invention leaked out to the Boche? The War Office's challenge was to maintain complete surprise.

"To achieve maximum effect, we need the enemy to believe H.G. Wells's Martians have landed. Under such pressure the tank unit itself was becoming jittery. To be quite honest, I saw the tank's need for secrecy as someone else's problem. My challenge was what to do about Pegasus.

"Then I remembered how, fourteen years ago, I appealed to your comrade, Mr. Sherlock Holmes, for help. I turned up again on his doorstep. Within minutes, he came up with a spectacular idea. We should deliberately leak word out that with *Project Pegasus* we were on the verge of a great break-through in training riders by the thousand for our cavalry regiments, that because of the Western Front in stalemate it was important for England to launch an aggressive war of manoeuvre in Ottoman territories."

Holmes took up the narrative. "The rumour," he explained, "would be so compelling, Berlin's spies would be diverted from anything else. There was one knotty problem. There wasn't a German spy left in the whole of England. On the day the war started, every known German agent and not a few innocent Prussian hairdressers and cabaret *artistes* had been rounded up. We needed to find – create, even – a traitor, someone Berlin would take seriously." Holmes pointed towards our last view of the Vickers. "By now you will have guessed that I suggested Colonel Moran as our man – someone who would sell out his country to Satan if the price was right. When Mason here put the idea to the landship people at the Admiralty, it tickled them pink. The question was, how to bring Moran into the game?

"Again I took Mr. Holmes's advice," added Mason. "I joined the Colonel's favourite Mayfair gambling joint, the Bagatelle Card Club. The War Office gave me substantial expenses. As often as possible, I sat in at his card table still wearing my uniform. In my cups, I let drop I was in charge of a secret military development – a highly secret development. The prototype had just passed its test with flying colours. The whole course of the war was about to change."

"But Mason," I protested, "for all you say about setting a trap, at this very moment..." and I pointed after the now invisible aeroplane, "...Moran's flying off with all the elements of your invention. Given the skill of Germany's mechanical engineers..."

"At this very moment, Watson," Holmes interrupted, "Moran is flying off to a secret rendezvous, yes, but with a crate containing parts for a perfectly useless mechanical horse. Some are authentic – a common or garden spring-balanced mechanism and the correct wheels instead of hoofs – but we've thrown in a dozen metal squares which look vital but have no purpose whatsoever. Mason's engineers deliberately overdosed on symmetry. All sorts of pre-drilled holes in the plates allow an infinity of ways to put it together, plus we've included an apologetic, official-looking note saying there has been a delay in manufacturing the 'active ingredient', which will be delivered as soon as possible. I wish there were such an ingredient, but there isn't. Germany's best mechanics will take months to figure out that once again they've been tricked by Perfidious Albion."

I stared in awed silence at the immense hulk of the landship and imagined what damage it could have done on my Regiment's behalf at the Battle of Maiwand those many years ago, where we lost so many men and almost every horse. It was time to drive back to the racecourse. "Major," I said, "I want to put a few guineas on the last race. Can you recommend something rather faster over the jumps than Pegasus?"

"I can, Doctor," came the reply. "A racing certainty by the name of Cinzano."

Arm in arm, the three of us walked back along the line of stables to the waiting Empress.

I was back at my medical practice in London's Marylebone District when a sealed letter arrived from John Mason:

Dear Dr. Watson,

The Vickers F.B.5 has been found. It was abandoned intact on a flat stretch in the Galloway Hills. The crofter who came across it reported seeing lights of a vessel close inshore. It steamed away at top speed. I think we can say Pegasus will soon be tucked up in her new stables in The Fatherland. No hint whatsoever of the 'tank' has leaked out. Two dozen or so are on their way to Amiens – mission accomplished.

I have applied for an honourable discharge from the ASC (on 'injury' grounds) and resigned from the Bagatelle Card Club! There's even talk of awarding me a medal, the new Silver War Badge. I wonder if our paths will ever cross again? I hope so. Either way, you and Mr. Holmes will always receive a warm welcome at the Stud whenever you are in the Shoscombe region.

John Mason

The End

The Captain in the Duke Of Wellington's Regiment

by Tim Symonds

I awoke to the first rays of the morning sun pouring through the bedroom window at 221b, Baker Street, my London lodgings. It was Tuesday, 22nd June, 1897. Celebrations for Queen Victoria's Diamond Jubilee were about to begin. A convoy carrying envoys and ambassadors and assorted European Royal Families would set off from Buckingham Palace at exactly 11:15, heralded by the firing of a cannon in Hyde Park. My old regiments, the 5th Northumberland Fusiliers and the 66th Berkshire Regiment of Foot, would be marching in the procession alongside Bengal Lancers and officers of the Indian Imperial Service in *kirtas* with gold sashes.

To catch a glimpse of Her Imperial Majesty meant that my comrade Sherlock Holmes and I would need to get into position early on. The clinking of test-tubes, pipettes, beakers, and Florence flasks and a malodorous stench seeping from Holmes's chemical bench told me that he was already up. I dressed quickly and hurried downstairs to the sitting room. Our landlady, Mrs. Hudson, had laid a fortifying breakfast on the table, together with her treasured pair of music hall glasses in brass with inlaid panels in tortoiseshell. I adjusted the lenses to my eye, picking out the patriotic 'VR' for *Victoria Regina* in bullet-pocks on our wall, a decorative bit of shooting practice by my fellow lodger in one of his periods of boredom. None of us could know that the binoculars were about to be critical in a case which would culminate with a more startling twist in the tail than any Holmes and I had ever encountered. It would bring back with a vengeance Holmes's remark that "*life is infinitely stranger than anything which the mind of man can invent...If we could fly out of that window...peep in at the odd things which are going on, the strange coincidences, the plannings, the cross-purposes, the wonderful chains of events...it would make all fiction, with its conventionalities and foreseen conclusions, most stale and unprofitable."*

We left Baker Street in good time to take command of a few square feet near Hyde Park Corner, at the foot of a great equestrian statue commemorating Field Marshall Wellesley's defeat of Napoleon at Waterloo. Behind us stood Apsley House, a record in honey-coloured limestone of Wellesley's power and social prominence on becoming the first Duke of Wellington. A ceremonial half-guard composed of six or seven men in the uniform of the Duke's Regiment was forming on the mansion's terrace, each soldier glancing through the barrel of his rifle to check for cleanliness. I turned the opera glasses on them. A tall, athletic man in captain's uniform came into focus. For a moment he looked my way. I gave an involuntary gasp. "Holmes," I exclaimed in stupefaction, "that soldier up there, the flaxen-haired man with the sunburned face in a captain's uniform. Isn't he remarkably like Giles Gilchrist, the student at the College of St. Luke's who tried to cheat his way to a scholarship?"

Before Holmes could take the glasses, a shout of "Fire!" came from Hyde Park, followed instantly by the roar of a cannon and a hundred-thousand throats. As one, we turned towards Constitution Hill to catch the first glimpse of Her Majesty rounding the corner. Moments later, the open royal coach with its diminutive figure dressed in black passed by. I swung the binoculars back to Apsley House. Like Banquo's ghost, the foot-soldiers and the captain with his Mark IV Martini-Henry rifle had gone.

My stupefaction at the chance sighting through Mrs. Hudson's binoculars derived from a case some two years earlier. I planned to publish it someday under the title 'The Adventure of the Three Students'. Holmes and I were on a visit to one of England's great university towns. Soon after settling into our lodgings we received an unexpected visit from a Mr. Hilton Soames, tutor and lecturer at St. Luke's College. He was in a state of uncontrollable agitation. He told us the morrow was the opening day of the examination for the Fortescue Scholarship. Great care had been taken to keep the questions secret. "I am one of the examiners," our visitor explained. "Three students are scheduled to take the examination: Gilchrist, an excellent student and athlete, together with a serious and peaceful Indian fellow, and a Scot, brilliant but lazy and dissipated. Each has rooms above my quarters.

"Yesterday afternoon," he continued, "when I came back to my study I came across the galley proofs scattered across the floor. One of the students must have found a way to enter my rooms and make a hurried transcription of the questions. Mr. Holmes," the tutor cried piteously. "A hideous scandal will ensue unless I find which of the three it was."

"Then you must call in the police, sir," I informed him.

"That I cannot do, Dr. Watson!" came the sharp reply. "When the law is evoked, it cannot be stayed. This is one of those cases where, for the credit of the college, it is most essential to avoid dishonour."

My comrade threw me a rueful glance and pushed himself up from the chair. The tutor led us the half-mile to the scene of the crime. Holmes set to work. "Ah-ha, Watson!" my comrade murmured. "We are getting a few cards in our hand."

A visit to the college athletic grounds confirmed his case. Gilchrist was the only one of the three students who could have been the culprit. Confronted the next morning by the three of us, the guilty student burst out to Soames, "I have a letter here which I wrote before I knew that my sin had found me out. Here it is, sir. You'll see that I have written, '*I have determined not to go in for the examination*'. I was recently offered a commission in the Colonial Police on a seven-year contract. If you agree to overlook my transgression, I shall go out to

Rhodesia on the next available berth and remain for the full term without once stepping foot back on these shores."

The plea was met by reluctant, if relieved, assent from Soames, whereupon Gilchrist insisted on shaking hands all round. At the door he halted for a last, melancholy look. He pointed at the tutor's bookshelves. "I shall miss *Thucydides* and the *Melian Dialogue*," he said. With a semblance of a smile, he added, "But most of all, I shall miss the Midsummer Carnival. I was credited by the girls with cutting a fine figure around the Maypole."

Confirmation of Gilchrist's departure for foreign shores came via the arrival of a postal card picturing a Castle Mail packet. It was franked in Suakin, a town on the Red Sea. The message struck a cheery note:

Dear Mr. Holmes,

Thanks to you and Dr. Watson, I am enjoying my very first trip on an ocean liner. The passage through the Suez Canal is proving especially enjoyable, accompanied as it is by reading a rollicking good Holmes-and-Watson tale in an old Strand Magazine *I came across in the ship's Library. It involves a fascinating adventuress. No need to tell you the adventure was '*A Scandal in Bohemia*'.*

Recalling this, it seemed highly unlikely Gilchrist could be the man in the uniform of an officer of the Duke of Wellingtons Regiment on the terrace at Apsley House. It must be a case of mistaken identity. I decided to put the matter out of my mind.

The days following the pomp and elation of the Diamond Jubilee were anticlimactic. Holmes spent the entire time in the sitting room. It was clear he was in urgent need of a new case. He hardly moved a muscle from morning to night, rousing himself now and then to fill the oldest and foulest of his pipes, only minutes later to tap out the lightly-singed tobacco and reach for a cigarette. Once in a while, as with a dog glancing at a well-gnawed bone, he would stare around at the familiar landmarks of our sitting room, the chemical corner and the acid-stained, deal-topped table, the row of formidable scrapbooks and books of reference, all the while making no effort to raise himself from the armchair into which he had sunk, even for meals.

Worse, the weather turned. The Tuesday sunshine gave way to a lowering Wednesday, to be repeated on the Thursday and Friday. With the return of fine weather on the Saturday, I could bear the air of torpor no longer. I reached for my bowler cap and cane. "Holmes," I called back from the landing, "I'm wandering down to W. H. Smith's to purchase a copy of the newspaper."

"And the *Police Gazette* if you will, Watson," came the languid response.

I left the news agent and strolled through Regents Park, dressed in its finest summer clothes, the various gardens awash with nannies pushing coach-built baby carriages among the delphiniums and begonias. I took possession of a bench overlooking the lake and turned to the lengthy description of Tuesday's events in *The Illustrated London News*. It began in portentous fashion:

> *Before the seventeen-carriage convoy carrying the royal family and leaders of Britain's dominions departed Buckingham Palace, Queen Victoria, with a touch of a button, sent an electronic message to her vast Empire: 'From my heart I thank my beloved people. May God bless them. V.R. & I." At exactly 11:15 a.m., a cannon fired in Hyde Park to announce the monarch's departure from the Palace. The roar of the cannon must have*

forced the clouds into retreat as the sun suddenly began to splash the streets of London. Eight cream horses pulled the Queen and Princess Christian of Schleswig-Holstein in an open carriage. Vendors hawked souvenir jubilee flags, mugs, and programmes. One lively group held up a banner declaring "Victoria – Queen of Earthly Queens".

A human fence of soldiers, their bayonets protruding like pickets, walled off the course of the six-mile procession. Despite the festive occasion, Victoria – in perpetual mourning for her beloved husband, Albert, and two of her children – was dressed in black. The colourful dress uniforms of the colonial forces, however, more than compensated for the monochrome monarch. The procession, which included representatives of all Empire nations, swept through Hyde Park Corner and onward to London's world-famous landmarks, such as Trafalgar Square, the National Gallery, London Bridge, and Big Ben. Safeguarded by a Metropolitan Police Special Branch Superintendent, Her Majesty returned to Windsor Castle, where she was greeted by dignitaries from the county of Buckingham and Slough.

I was about to turn to the *Police Gazette* when a dispatch headed '*Spectator Struck by Bullet*' caught my eye. It went on –

A most unfortunate event occurred near Hyde Park Corner at the commencement of the Jubilee procession when a member of the public was killed by a bullet in the head. His body was found in a carriage by the side of the route. The shot must have occurred at the exact moment the cannon went off nearby. This would explain why no-one in the vicinity appeared to take note. The trajectory may have been the result of a ricochet from a salute of rifles through the inadvertent use of live ammunition. According to identity papers found on him, the deceased was a member of a special unit of the North-Eastern Rhodesia Police concerned with wild-life preservation. Inspector G. Lestrade of Scotland Yard is investigating. The Inspector is renowned for his success in numerous cases. An explanation is expected soon.

Even before reaching the end of the account, I was on my feet. "My Heavens!" I cried out, "*A member of a special unit of the North-Eastern Rhodesia Police.*" – the very Force Gilchrist had gone out to join. My mind flashed back to Apsley House and the figure of the captain in the Duke of Wellington's Regiment. The Ceremonial half-guard would have had a clear line of sight from the top of the building to a stationary carriage at Hyde Park Corner.

I set off, my pace quickening until I was positively running. I was perplexed. If the apparition truly was Gilchrist, why was he dressed in a military uniform and not the Dress uniform of a Colonial policeman? Why would he order anyone to shoot someone from the very same police force he had gone to Africa to join? In any case, it would take great skill to hit a man in the head at such a distance.

I left the Park and hailed a brougham. "Cabbie," I shouted, "Apsley House, if you please, at the double!" A moment later I called out, "First, take me to 221, Baker Street." I would change into my old Medical officer's uniform brought back from Afghanistan, replete with indelible stains of blood from the fatal battle of Maiwand. On previous occasions my army uniform proved a useful entrée when brother officers were around.

There was no sign of Holmes. I dropped the *Police Gazette* on his chair, changed clothes, and returned to the waiting cabbie.

I left the cab on Park Lane and approached Apsley House from the side. A solitary guard in the uniform of the Duke of Wellington's Regiment stood at the Tradesmen's entrance. He gave a nod of recognition at my former rank and was happy to answer my questions, "Yes, sir," he replied, "I was one of the ceremonial guard on the roof. Six of us and the Captain."

I asked, "You were there from the start?"

"From about half-an-hour before the cannon went off."

"Then what?"

"Then we stood down."

"The Captain," I pursued. "Has he been your commanding officer long?"

The soldier shook his head. "No, sir. Our regular commanding officer's on furlough. This captain appeared from nowhere. And we haven't seen him since. He told us he spent the last two years in Africa helping the Mashonaland Field Force. They'd been hard against it, putting down a native rebellion."

The soldier pointed at his rifle. "It explained why he had a Martini-Henry with him while the rest of the Regiment has these Mark 1 Magazine Lee-Enfields and cordite cartridges."

"Continue," I urged.

"Not much more to it, sir. He gave orders to bring blank cartridges and form a sort of make-shift Honour Guard on the roof eleven o'clock sharp."

"So all of you were issued with blanks, are you sure?"

"Yes, sir. Why would we want live ammo?"

"No one hesitated at carrying out his orders?"

"Of course not, sir. We could see he was an officer."

So by eleven o'clock, you've formed up on the roof – "

"That's right, sir. The cannon in Hyde Park was to go off at 11:15 precisely. We were to pull the trigger the very second it went off. I can tell you, it wasn't the cannon going off which didn't 'arf give me a fright. It was the Captain firing off that Martini-Henry right behind me. A ruddy great cloud of black soot came swirling around my legs. You see, he wasn't standing in the line-up. He took up a position behind us."

On my return Mrs. Hudson was waiting for me at the foot of the stairs with a letter from the last delivery of the day. It was from Hilton Soames at St. Luke's, the very person who had first brought us into contact with Giles Gilchrist. Holmes had returned. I read the letter to him, emphasising the underlinings.

Dear Dr. Watson,

I am in a state of <u>great agitation</u>. I hope you will intervene with Mr. Holmes on my behalf. I spied Gilchrist here yesterday. He was dressed in the uniform of an officer in a British regiment. Yes, I know, it <u>does</u> seem fanciful. However, I have an excellent eye for faces and <u>I am sure it was he</u>. If so, the rascal has broken his word to stay out of England for the length of his commission. Given his unpalatable behaviour two years ago and the present use of a uniform to which he is almost certainly not entitled, I worry he may be up to no good.

To confirm that I was not mistaken, I ordered one of my students to follow the man in question to his hotel. The student heard him tell the other guests he planned to "have a go" for a stuffed toy at the shooting gallery tomorrow afternoon – the Midsummer Carnival commences then. He signed the register with the name 'Douglas Stanyon'. If it <u>is</u> Gilchrist, the resort to an alias clearly indicates <u>he wishes to disguise his presence</u>, either because of the dishonour he very nearly brought to St. Luke's good name, or because he's up to no good. I am nervous for my well-being. He may well hold a grudge against me. I implore you and Mr. Holmes to take the early morning express. In that hope, I shall be on the platform to greet you.

I remain, yours very sincerely,

H. Soames.

P.S. Come with fishing tackle. I understand you are enthusiastic fly fishermen. The Windrush at Witney holds a big head of wild Brown Trout. College anglers tell me an eight-foot rod for a four or five-weight floating line is ideal.

The letter galvanised my comrade. He sprang from the armchair in which he had spent much of the previous four days. "There's an inducement, Watson – trout for supper – but first we must be there when this 'Captain Stanyon' pays a visit to the Carnival shooting gallery. If the man in the carriage was killed from atop Apsley House, whoever pulled the trigger would need to be a very good shot indeed. I recall a breeze from the north. The wind would have moved the bullet almost three inches to the left at two-hundred yards."

We boarded a first-class carriage on the morning express, a formidable litter of rods, reels, and baskets perched on the rack above us. Soames was awaiting our arrival with a brougham at the ready. It took us to the Carnival. It was, the tutor told us, the six hundred and eighty sixth mid-summer carnival to be held without interruption since the reign of King John. He led us to the shooting gallery. A tall, bronzed figure in the day dress of a Colonial Police force officer was being handed a rifle by the woman in charge. Rows of small metal ducks trundled at a good pace from one side to the other, alternating rows revolving in opposite directions. Slightly to the rear a wheel rotated clay pipes at around twenty revolutions per minute. On one side an exotic Tibetan Rising Gong dangled from an ebony stand for atmosphere.

Duck after duck was knocked over by the Winchester Model 1890 in the shooter's hand until the magazine's fifteen cartridges were spent. "Good Lord, Holmes," I muttered *sotto voce*, deeply impressed, "if that's Gilchrist – and we can now see it can't be anyone else – he's certainly learnt to shoot."

"As you say," Holmes returned, "but we must push him a little further."

My companion stepped forward. Gilchrist greeted him, beckoning the woman to reload the Winchester and bring another rifle for Holmes.

"So not unexpectedly we meet again, Mr. Holmes," he said in a somewhat guarded tone. "I should have guessed Dr. Watson spotted me. He kept the glasses on me a second too long. I was also pretty certain Soames was behind the fellow checking the register at The Randolph Hotel."

Like a Roman orator, he turned to address the gaggle of onlookers: "Dear friends and countrymen! You may have heard of this person standing next to me. His name is Mr. Sherlock Holmes. They say he's as skilled with a rifle as the famous White Hunter Alan Black, author of *Hunting in Somaliland with the 3rd Baron Delamere*, but we must put that to the test, must we not?" A small cheer went up.

The woman held out the two loaded rifles, a Colt Lightning alongside the Winchester. Gilchrist waved a hand.

"As my guest, Mr. Holmes, you may take first pick."

Holmes gave a quizzical look. He asked, "You have no preference between the two makes?"

"No," came Gilchrist's reply, "but if it's all the same to you, I'll stick with the rifle I've just been using."

He took the Winchester, touched his tongue with a forefinger and placed a bead of saliva on the front sight. "Ready, steady, go!" Gilchrist called out to the gallery attendant. The ducks began to whirl. "Faster!" Gilchrist ordered. The woman increased the speed. Even though the ducks were now whizzing round in a blur neither shooter missed his target. Nine shots in, Gilchrist and Holmes turned their sights on the revolving clay pipes. Each knocked over six with six shots. The shooting display was all over in twenty seconds. Gilchrist started to lower the Winchester. With a sudden sharp movement Holmes swung the Colt towards the Tibetan Gong and fired. The bullet smacked into the metal, like a musical punctuation mark. The gaggle of spectators gave a sharp clap of hands.

"Know your guns, sir," Holmes advised the astonished Gilchrist. "The Winchester Model 1890 in your hand fires fifteen cartridges. The Colt Lightning carbine fires sixteen."

A chastened Gilchrist replied, "Mr. Holmes, you are indeed remarkably knowledgeable on such weaponry."

At which Holmes returned, "In turn, I can vouch for your shooting skills, Gilchrist – to be able to collar a man at two-hundred yards with a Mark IV Martini-Henry from the roof of Number One, London. The question is why?"

The whizzing lines of ducks came to an abrupt stop. The woman picked up the rifles. "Sorry, gentlemen," she said with a shrug. "You've burnt out the electric motor."

She handed each of the two men a silky Mohair stuffed elephant.

We left the Midsummer Carnival and repaired to a quiet corner in Gilchrist's hotel. His elephant sat by his side. "Cigarette, gentlemen?" Gilchrist exclaimed, extending a gold cigarette case first to Holmes, then to me, and finally to Soames.

I confronted him with my belief he had murdered a fellow member of the North-Eastern Rhodesian Police force. Though appearing to accept the charge against him, Gilchrist seemed intent on testing it. "Dr. Watson," he continued, "every bit of what you say is circumstantial. You spotted someone looking extraordinarily like me on a terrace at Apsley House, dressed in a captain's uniform. Goodness me! London is the stamping-ground of the entire Duke of Wellington's Regiment. You say this fellow was holding a Mark IV Martini-Henry rifle? That model has been in service almost ten years to the day. There are thousands of them out there, somewhere or other." His expression turned derisive. "Such testimony would hardly be permitted in a Court of Law, especially for a capital offence!" He pointed at Hilton Soames. "As to my former tutor's poor opinion of my character..."

Holmes intervened. "Gilchrist – or Captain Stanyon, whichever you prefer – I spend a great deal of time at the Old Bailey. Yes, testimony regarding your character might be deemed inadmissible. Evidence in the form of eyewitnesses or documents carries the greater authority, as you imply, but not all secondary evidence will be dismissed. You would be wise not to underestimate the body of facts Dr. Watson has assembled."

The young man shifted uneasily.

"Go on, Mr. Holmes," he said. "You get more and more interesting."

Holmes continued, "The quality of such evidence goes only to weight and not to admissibility. Dr. Watson and I plan a return to Apsley House. The soldier Dr. Watson spoke to from the ceremonial guard will identify you. The same soldier will confirm you were armed with a Martini-Henry, the Mark IV, and it was fired by you from behind him – his ears took a day to stop ringing. The blast of black smoke didn't go up into the air at a forty-five degree angle as you might expect. It went past the soldier's legs on a trajectory which would take a bullet straight at the carriage where the body of your colleague was found."

Holmes pointed up at the ceiling. "You may claim such evidence would not be admissible in a Court of Law. I beg to differ. Even as we speak, your rooms are being searched by the management. No-one with your attachment to the Martini-Henry would throw it into the Serpentine River. I'm sure the rifle will be found, perhaps under a convenient loose floor-board, the Randolph being an ancient hotel."

Gilchrist watched us in silence. The seconds ticked past. "Heavens, he's going to make a run for it!" I thought. Finally, to general astonishment, he broke into a genial smile and said, "Well, I see no alternative – I confess! Murder was my reason for being on the terrace. Yes, the Martini-Henry is tucked away in my room. It was I who fired at the wretched fellow in the carriage. And if you like, gentlemen, I shall tell you why!"

The young man regaled us with a most extraordinary tale. Soon after he took up his post with the North-Eastern Rhodesia Police he had been assigned to a remote area to get experience of the testing life of the Bush. He came across an elderly White Hunter named Bill Powys, hot on the trail of an especially big tusker. Gilchrist realised the man was hunting Big Game without permission.

"In short, he was an ivory poacher," Gilchrist explained, "and making a fortune at it."

To avoid arrest, the hunter invited Gilchrist to join in the hunt. The offer was accepted.

"We bagged that old tusker and a couple more besides," Gilchrist related. "From then on, I spent all my spare hours with the old timer. Sometimes we would shoot four or five elephants at a go."

It was not long before Gilchrist's skill with a heavy rifle equalled and surpassed that of his companion.

"Then one day something happened – a terrible thing at the time," our narrator continued. "Old Bill got himself killed. We were too close to a cow-herd. The wind turned and they charged. Some people think elephants can remember ivory poachers. Whether they could or not, they certainly exacted revenge. Bill's old legs must have given away. He stumbled. The herd trampled him into the earth."

Gilchrist continued to poach ivory. He hired three or four natives to remove the tusks. "Better them than me. Damnable

138

hard work in the heat. You see, a third of the tusk is below the gum line. To get at it you have to cut open the skull."

The demand for ivory was ceaseless. Soon he assembled a whole gang, ready to take his orders. "We expanded into shooting rhino for their horn. Chappies in the Far East can't get enough of the stuff. Meant to be an aphrodisiac of some sort. Make tea out of it, I'm told. For months things went along perfectly well until a *boykie* by the name of Behari Das joined the Force. They let him in because he said he'd been in the police in India. As it turned out, he became a perfect nuisance. He took it upon himself to bring the poaching to an end – as assiduous about it as those missionaries out there to save souls.

"The fellow kept on about the Hindu god Ganesh having the head of an elephant," Gilchrist continued. "I evaded him by shifting constantly from one part of the Bush to another. I even crossed the border into South Zambezia. Then, a few months ago something put the wind up me. Behari Das walked into my office, looked me straight in the eye and said, "You know, Assistant Inspector Gilchrist, I think we're barking up the wrong gum-tree."

"Are we?" I enquired as casually as possible.

"Yes," he replied. "All this time I've been on the look-out for a local leading the gang of ivory poachers, an African."

"And now?" I asked.

"I am sure it's a white man"."

Gilchrist burst into sardonic laughter. "It was at that second, my dear audience, that the *boykie* awoke the Grim Reaper. I wasn't going to have someone do me out of my fun, to say nothing of the fortune I've been accruing. A few days later I learnt the fellow was coming to London, but he was incredibly secretive as to why. Wouldn't tell anyone. I put two and two together and decided he was planning to go over the heads of his superiors in the North-Eastern Rhodesia Police to report me to the Colonial Office itself. I knew at once what I had to do. I couldn't take any chances. I would follow him and dispatch him."

He bowed his head, staring at the floor. Then, as though accepting his fate, he addressed my comrade. "Mr. Holmes, surely I warrant more than the ministrations of a local bobby! I came across the name of a Scotland Yard detective in *The Illustrated London News* – Inspector Lestrade. Why not contact him right away? If you and Dr. Watson and Mr. Soames are content to leave me here in the comfort of The Randolph, you have my word I won't move an inch until he arrives to effect my arrest. What's more, I shall use the time to write out a full confession. Is it a deal?"

A slight smile flickered around Holmes's lips at the young man's effrontery. "Watson," he said, turning to me, "I see no reason why not. Lestrade would appreciate the credit, and an airing away from the fog will do him good. We'll take our friend here at his word, though with a caveat that within the hour Dr. Watson will telegraph a *Hue and Cry Notice* to every port in Britain asking the Docks police to be on the *qui vive* for a man of your description, known to personate an officer in the Duke of Wellington's Regiment. If you are spotted trying to escape your just desserts, they are to hold you come what may."

I looked over at Hilton Soames. He stared at his former student for several moments before shrugging his shoulders in nervous acquiescence.

Over dinner, I watched Holmes picking at his plate. "You know, Watson," he said, "I'm feeling rather sorry for the lad. Two years ago Nemesis in the shape of Sherlock Holmes forced a college student to abandon his hope of becoming a great Classics professor. Disgraced, the student set off like Conrad's Marlow into the blank spaces of Darkest Africa. Little did he know that in distant India, Nemesis was again stirring her loins in the shape of Behari Das. Gilchrist's fresh start and financial well-being as an elephant hunter – even his liberty – was under threat when Behari Das turned up in Rhodesia."

We departed from the university town to spend two enjoyable days on the Windrush between Witney and Burford. Without waders at our disposal, we cast our lines upstream from a position on the bank. The two of us returned to Baker Street with the basket filled to the brim with Brown Trout and half-a-dozen Grayling with brilliantly coloured dorsal fins.

It was after one of Mrs. Hudson's famed afternoon teas of oat cakes with chunks of hearty cheese, smoked salmon, and homemade chutney when my attention was caught by a man on the opposite pavement. I had taken up a familiar position, cigarette in hand, staring out of the spacious window at the rush-and-tumble of Baker Street below.

"Holmes," I called back into the room, "there's someone lurking in front of the haberdasher's shop-window. He has his back to us, but I'm sure it's Inspector Lestrade."

Holmes crossed to my side. "Our friend looks even more furtive than usual," he agreed. "What's more absurd, he's disguising himself in a waterproof coat with a detachable cape more suited to the depth of winter than high summer."

The man's assumed nonchalance was being put at risk by the derision of the Baker Street Irregulars, a group of street-urchins in newsboy caps employed once-in-a-while by Holmes at a shilling a day (plus expenses) to gather information. A set of sharp cuffs from the object of their attention sent them scattering.

"What do you suppose Lestrade's doing here on Baker Street?" I asked. "It seems a long way to come from Scotland Yard's premises to buy a handkerchief or a pair of green suspenders!"

"I doubt if he's eyeing the goods on display, Watson," Holmes replied. "I myself have made use of the reflection in that same shop window to keep an eye on this side of the street, specifically our own front door."

"Why would he do that?" I asked. "Why not knock and get shown up as usual by Mrs. Hudson?"

Holmes held up his briar. "I have enough tobacco in this pipe for another fifteen minutes. I wager we'll have the answer before it runs out – I suspect he's waiting to see if we have a visitor."

Our vigil was short. Well before the quarter-hour, the sharp sound of equid hooves came through the open window. Wheels grated against the curb, followed by a pull at the bell. A quick glance showed Lestrade was still across the street, though he had now turned full-face. Moments later, a flushed Hilton Soames was ushered into our front room. He threw himself forward, holding out a piece of paper torn from a note-book.

"Mr. Holmes, I received this message! It came this morning. I haven't the faintest idea what it means.. Once more, I beg for your help."

After the briefest glance at the note my comrade passed it to me with "Watson, what do you make of that?" A curious, almost satisfied look had come into the deep-set grey eyes.

The writing was hurried but legible, the punctuation flowery, the grammar punctilious:

> To *WHOMSOEVER steams this open: I hope you are as edified at the accompanying letter as I am over having to write it!!*

The size of individual letters, the degree and regularity of slanting, angularity, ornamentation, and curvature were identical to the writing on the postal card sent by Giles Gilchrist from the Egyptian Sudan two years earlier.

Holmes held out a hand to the tutor. "And the letter he mentions, please."

"That's the very reason I'm here," Soames replied excitably. "I don't have it!" He dipped a hand into a pocket and drew out an envelope. "I only have the note and this. As you can see, it was delivered to the College addressed to me. I am certain the writing's Gilchrist's." He paused. "Oh, hello, Dr. Watson – I'm sorry to barge in on you, but it's the most damnable thing – there was nothing else in the envelope except that slip of paper."

"Show me the envelope," Holmes ordered. After a single glance he muttered, "Postmarked '*Holborn and St. Pancras*'. A significant clue to the sender's travel plans, don't you agree, Watson?" He passed the envelope back to Soames. "The author of the note anticipated correctly. This envelope has indeed been steamed open. Although addressed to you, someone else got there first."

Holmes seemed to be sniffing a scent, like a trained bloodhound.

"What do you make of it?" I asked.

He pointed at the window. "Five guineas to your one we'll not have to wait long before the present beneficiary of the letter reveals himself."

Even as he spoke, we heard an authoritative rap on the front door, followed by the firm, rapid step of one who knew well the ground upon which he walked. Our door was flung open.

"Mr. Soames," Holmes called out, "may I introduce Inspector Lestrade of the Yard. I have no doubt it was he who arranged for the letter to be purloined."

Holmes turned to address the newcomer. "Inspector, if I'm not mistaken, you knew that Mr. Soames was on his way here and – knowing when his train was due to arrive – you waited across the street before joining us.

Lestrade scowled but nodded, and Holmes continued. "Are you here to bring us up to date on the life and times of young Gilchrist, starting with the stolen letter?"

143

"'Stolen' is a little harsh, Mr. Holmes," the inspector chortled. "The beadle at St Luke's...(he paused, looking with some embarrassment at Soames)...intercepted it. On my authority," he added hurriedly. "We suspected that Mr. Gilchrist might be in touch."

As Lestrade spoke, his hand went into a pocket. It reappeared holding a letter some three pages in length. With a sense of ceremony kindled by our keen attention, he began reading aloud:

The Randolph, June 30. Midnight

My dear Soames,

You and the others have gone. As I compose this letter, Inspector Lestrade must be on his way from the Yard. Unfortunately I shall not be here to greet him. Yes, my dear former Tutor and Lecturer, I know. My Scottish grandfather used to say "O kingis word shuld be o kingis bonde", *and like the kings I did give my word, but I must be clear − my word is my bond except when it becomes a necessary tool to free myself from uncomfortable situations. I was brought up to be charming, not sincere. It's easy for you or others to preach. One cannot see all one's hopes, all one's plans, about to be shattered for a second time in as many years and make no effort to save them. What was it the versifier Kipling wrote −* 'If you can dream − and not make dreams your master; If you can think − and not make thoughts your aim; If you can meet with Triumph and Disaster, And treat those two impostors just the same...'.

Well, I can't treat those twin imposters just the same. I think you would agree being arrested for murder can be deemed uncomfortable, at least equal to the anathema of being cast out of St. Luke's for cheating. If my student peccadilloes mean I can never have a seat at the High Table of a famous College, isn't that punishment enough for one life-time? Facing a sudden and ignominious end to an adventurous life in the heart of Africa was too much. You heard Mr. Holmes make mock of my predicament. He warned me that within the hour Dr. Watson would telegraph a Hue and Cry poster to every sea-port with details of my appearance – height, posture, eye-colour, name, and pseudonym. It was a challenge that – even as I write – I am preparing to meet! By the time you receive this letter, I shall again have demonstrated the power of dress to obscure purpose, which I discovered so happily at Apsley House as a captain in the fabled Duke of Wellington's. You ask, if I escape every clutch, where shall I go? I shall tell you. The Far East emits her siren calls. A year or two in the Lesser Sunda Islands among yellow-tongued dragons more than ten feet long tickles my fancy.

With all the possibilities inherent in life, I Am,
Yours etc., etc.

G. Gilchrist.

P.S. I shall miss my confiscated Martini-Henry. Please let Mr. Sherlock Holmes know that 'Captain Stanyon' will be replacing it with a Colt Large Frame Lightning taking the .50-95 Express. And let him know he is welcome to my spanking new captain's uniform. I am leaving it for him here at The Randolph Hotel.

Soames let out a screech. "He speaks of '*Peccadilloes*'! Peccadilloes is hardly the description I would use!" he gasped.

"So, Lestrade," I said, "the man fled. Did my *Hue and Cry Notice* have any result at all? Has Gilchrist been apprehended? If so, shall we be needed at his trial?"

A watchful tone crept into the inspector's reply. "Thanks to your *Hue and Cry*, and some further valuable assistance from Mr. Holmes here, our men had no trouble apprehending Gilchrist – at the Albert Docks. As to a trial..."

Soames jumped back in. "Then you *have* apprehended Gilchrist! Wonderful! Wonderful! Does the wretch lie rotting in one of Her Majesty's gaols? Is he waiting to be hanged at Newgate? Will his body be buried in an unmarked grave within the walls?"

Lestrade tried to hide a guffaw by a solemn shake of the head. "No, no, and no to your questions, Mr. Soames, I'm sorry to say," he declared. "Gentlemen, I must make something plain. Gilchrist was apprehended but he was not held. He is no longer in custody. What's more, he'll get away scatheless. There will never be a trial. He was – deliberately – allowed to board a liner to the South Pacific."

"How is that possible?" I exclaimed. "After all, he confessed to cold-blooded murder!"

"He did, Dr. Watson, yes," came the discomfited reply, "but I repeat, he will never be brought to trial."

"Now listen, Lestrade," I remonstrated angrily, "a Colonial Police officer is killed in broad daylight right here in our capital city. You had the perpetrator in your clutches and you released him. What of justice! What of Behari Das's grieving family?"

The police inspector's gaze went from one to other of us before settling back on Holmes. "I accept that all in this room deserve an explanation. Mr. Holmes is the one to provide it, since he's the man who worked out how to put together all the pieces. The plot can be revealed on the strictest terms but you must each give your sworn word you will not publish an account of a case which involves the attempted assassination of our Imperial Majesty until she herself passes into the Great Beyond."

Soames and I gawped. "The attempted assassination of our Queen?" we chorused.

Lestrade inclined his head. "Yes. Didn't I mention the heavy parcel in Behari Das's hands when his body was found?"

"You did not, Inspector," I informed him.

"Over to you, Mr. Holmes," said Lestrade.

My friend settled back in his chair. "Mr. Soames, I have an elder brother, Mycroft, a veritable spider at the beating heart of the British Government. The moment we began our investigation into the shooting, I informed Mycroft and thanks to my bother the India Office made Scotland Yard privy to confidential information about Behari Ras."

"That information being?" Soames asked.

"First, let me deal with your former student," Holmes said. "He followed Behari Das to London, believing that he was about to tell a tale of illicit ivory poaching activities to the Colonial Secretary. To Gilchrist, it would mean being kicked out of the North-Eastern Rhodesian Police and suffering the loss of a very considerable income from tusks and horns, and possibly enduring a large fine and a year or two in Fort Jameson's mosquito-ridden gaol. As it turns out, Behari Das came to London for an entirely different reason."

I opened my mouth to speak but Holmes's hand went up quickly. "Patience, Watson! I assure you I shall get to that. But first, on June 27th, a corpse was discovered near Hyde Park Corner. A heavy bullet had taken away the back of his head. This is when Scotland Yard came into the picture. Watson, I passed on your report of seeing Gilchrist on the terrace. They too realised the perfect spot for a shooter was the terrace of Apsley House although it lay a good two-hundred yards away."

"Until then," added Lestrade, "we had no idea who might have pulled the trigger, nor a motive. I immediately got in touch with the British Colonial Administrator out in Africa, a man by the name of Codrington. I asked whether Gilchrist could have put a bullet into a man's forehead at that distance. If not, your suspicions, Doctor, would fall apart."

Lestrade reached into a pocket and held up a telegram.

"You'll be impressed with Codrington's reply. Two months ago, a competition was held in Chirisa, in the north of the country. A coterie of shooters paid fifty pounds for a single-day licence to kill Big Game and a chance to win a silver cup the size of an elephant egg. Each could decide for himself which of the 'Big Five' to kill – elephant, lion, rhino, leopard and, most dangerous of all, Cape buffalo. There was an important stipulation – each hunter was limited to five cartridges. Some returned with an elephant and a lion or two. Only one hunter returned having bagged all five targets." The inspector asked rhetorically, "Well, gentlemen, any guesses as to...?"

Impatient, I interrupted, "Holmes, you said that it turns out Behari Das came to England for an entirely different reason. Are you telling us the dead man was *not* in London to spill the beans on Gilchrist?"

"Correct, Watson. He was not," came the reply.

"So he was here simply to celebrate Her Majesty's Diamond Jubilee?"

Holmes gave an odd smile. "Not quite," he answered. "This brings us to the parcel. Why had he kept such a heavy package so close to him – on his lap – merely to sit waiting for Her Majesty's coach to pass by? Why not leave it at his hotel with the rest of his possessions – clothing and shoes, etcetera? Before the authorities opened the package, they noticed a few unusual features about it. The string was secured by three knots. In India this symbolises three aspects of commitment –

manasa, *vachaar*, and *karmana*: '*Believing it*', '*Saying it*', and '*Executing it*'. And there was the matter of the parcel's weight."

Unable to restrain myself I burst out, "Surely you're not telling us it was – "

" – a bomb? Yes, Doctor. Behari Das planned to hurl a powerful explosive at Her Majesty. A half-pound of gelignite, with a fuse designed to detonate on impact."

At my side, Soames piped up, "But why would anyone want to kill Queen Victoria?"

Lestrade reached into a trouser pocket and brought out a florin. After a brief glance at the coin he flicked it to the tutor.

"Why are you giving me this?" Soames asked.

"You're a tutor in the Classics," came Lestrade's reply. "Take a look at the Latin inscription on the obverse side."

"*Victoria d.g. Britt. Reg. f.d.*," Soames read aloud. He looked up at the inspector. "So?" he asked.

Lestrade glanced at Holmes, who asked, "The date of the coin, Soames?"

Soames turned it this way and that. "*MDCCCLXX11*," he replied. "1872."

Again Lestrade dipped a hand in his pocket. He withdrew a second florin, checking it before sending it sailing through the air.

"And the Latin abbreviations on that second florin, Mr. Soames?"

"*Victoria Dei Gra. Britt. Regina Fid. Def. Ind. Imp*," the tutor read out.

"And the date?" Lestrade asked.

"*MDCCCXCIII*. 1893," the Classics Tutor replied.

"Twenty-one years later than the first florin. That '*Ind. Imp*' wasn't on the earlier coin," Lestrade pointed out. "Our Queen became Empress of India in 1877. Our deceased Indian friend might not quibble so much with '*Victoria by the Grace of God, Queen of the British territories, Defender of the Faith*'. He would react violently to '*Ind. Imp*' – '*Empress of India*'. When I informed

149

Mr. Holmes about the bomb, he consulted his elder brother Mycroft. That did the trick. Both Messrs. Holmes realised the name used by the assassin-to-be – Behari Ras – was a pseudonym. Enquiries revealed his real name was Bankim Bharathy Ramakrishna, a sergeant in the Bengal Police until he became implicated in an attempt to assassinate the British Political Agent. He changed his name and fled to Central Africa. While still Bharathy Ramakrishna, he became a follower of Bal Gangadhar Tilak, the man known to the Raj as 'the father of Indian unrest'.

"Tilak preaches *Swaraj*," continued Holmes. "It espouses independence from British rule – Independence, and at any cost. According to the Hindu scripture *Bhagavad Gita* no blame can be attached if you kill an oppressor without thought of reward – regicide included. In short, Behari Das was *not* in London to expose Gilchrist as an ivory poacher, nor to be one of a hundred thousand ordinary spectators at the Royal procession. He was here to fulfil a destiny – to help Mother India break loose from British rule."

Did Scotland Yard knew anything of the man's intentions before he arrived in England? I asked Lestrade.

"Not a thing," the Inspector replied. "The day before the Jubilee procession, completely by chance, a Special Branch Superintendent assigned to the Royal Family by the name of Melville was on the look-out for a band of French and Russian anarchists. He spotted our Indian friend leaving a side-entrance of the Autonomie Club, a favourite meeting place of Continental conspirators, some of them expert bomb-makers. The man had a parcel on his shoulder. He looked furtive. Melville was perfectly aware that assassins do not come solely from Ireland or the Continent. They also exist in large numbers throughout the Indian sub-Continent.

"Regrettably, the superintendent was given the slip. By contrast, Gilchrist was not to be shaken off – all that stalking after tigers no doubt. As he told you at The Randolph, he observed his quarry hiring a carriage and followed him to Hyde Park Corner. Gilchrist cast an eye around. He spotted Apsley House."

"All the while," explained Holmes, "like a trap-door spider, Behari Das was lying in wait for Her Majesty. The police found a sketch in a hidden pocket, showing the sons of the Maharajahs of Kuch and Behar, the Minister of Hyderabad, and the Prince of Gondal in the coach immediately preceding the Queen's. That coach was to be the signal for Behari Das to leap out, plunge through the line of soldiers, and fling the bomb into Her Majesty's lap. As it happened, he never got the chance."

"Do we know how Gilchrist got hold of the officer's uniform at such short notice?" I asked.

"Dege and Skinner on Savile Row," explained the inspector, "and very pricey too. Gilchrist must have bumped into the Duke of Wellington's Regiment in Central Africa. He told the tailors he'd returned from a hardship post to take part in the Jubilee procession, losing his uniform when a fire broke out in the ship's baggage hold. They worked through the night for such a patriotic young officer."

Soames burst out, "Then if Gilchrist hadn't shot the assassin dead, Her Majesty would have been blown to pieces less than ten minutes later!"

"Lucky for Special Branch, wasn't it!" Holmes responded drily. "They had charge of Her Majesty's safety."

"Nevertheless, Lestrade," I exclaimed, "we still haven't heard why you had Gilchrist in cuffs and then let him go!"

"Dr. Watson," came the rueful reply, "look at it from Special Branch's perspective. How could they let it go to trial in open court? The Queen's life had been put at serious risk. If it became public knowledge Superintendent Melville had the man in his sights yet was given the slip, he would become the laughing stock of the nation. It would mean an end to a meritorious career, even to Special Branch itself. That would free the Irish Fenian Brotherhood to try their hand at will.

"No, gentlemen," Lestrade ended, looking pointedly at the *VR* outlined in bullet-pocks on our wall, "after the Home Secretary spoke to a certain personage at a certain Norman castle in the county of Berkshire, we humble mortals at Scotland Yard were ordered in no uncertain terms to let Gilchrist go scot-free on giving his word he would once more quit England. A word one of my best officers is enforcing by accompanying him until the ship leaves Cape Town for its destination the other side of the world."

"Lestrade," I returned, "I take your point about *manasa*, *vachaar*, and *karmana*, and so on, but you also said the weight of the parcel was a give-away. Two four-ounce sticks of gelignite could hardly be called heavy, any more than half-a-pound of sausages or eight ounces of goose-feathers."

"Depends if the sausages or goose-feathers were wrapped in nuts, bolts, and ball bearings to inflict greater casualties than the blast by itself," came the reply.

We walked our guests to the top of the stairs and bid them *adieu*. In a voice breaking with emotion, Soames told Holmes, "Two years ago you came to my aid like *dikē*, the Greek goddess of moral justice. In view of the present events, but for your chance presence at the time of the Fortescue Scholarship affair, I wonder if I would still be here. Would I have met the terrible fate Gilchrist meted out to Behari Das?"

In a moment, I heard the front door bang behind them. I returned to the open window. Lestrade's hand was held out to Soames for the return of the two florins. Together the pair turned towards the Underground station and disappeared from our line of sight.

I looked back into the sitting room. "Holmes," I said, "I have a question. Lestrade gave you credit for Gilchrist's apprehension at the Albert Docks."

"I did make a small suggestion, yes," came a reply, the words muffled by a fresh pipe clenched in his teeth.

"May I know what?"

My comrade crossed to a line of books. Between *The Origin of Tree Worship* and my *Handy Guide to the Turf* he came to a compilation of twelve of our previous cases. Long, bony fingers flicked through the pages. "Ah, here, Watson, in your very own words:

> *Holmes disappeared into his bedroom and returned in a few minutes in the character of an amiable and simple-minded Nonconformist clergyman. His broad black hat, his baggy trousers, his white tie, his sympathetic smile, and general look of peering and benevolent curiosity were such as the great actor Mr. John Hare alone could have equalled.*

"Of course!" I shouted. "The postal card Gilchrist sent us. He was reading 'A Scandal in Bohemia' while his ship sailed through the Suez Canal. You must have pointed that out to Lestrade!"

Holmes chuckled. "A scriptural habit is a fine disguise until it turns out every police force in the country is looking for someone dressed like that. Nevertheless, England is mother to a myriad sea-ports. The Albert Docks are but one. Lestrade's men had to arrive at the docks in very short time."

"How do you suppose they managed that?" I asked.

"From the postmark on the envelope."

"'*Holborn and St. Pancras*'?" I queried. "What did that tell them?"

"It told *me* that Gilchrist posted the letter within spitting distance of Euston Station. And where would trains from Euston take you? To Northampton, Coventry, Birmingham, Wolverhampton, Stoke-on-Trent, Macclesfield, Stockport, Manchester, Runcorn...and Liverpool, the site of the Albert Docks. If you want to escape unnoticed, which better port than one from which a hundred emigrant packets a month sail to every quarter of the Earth?"

I checked my watch. Six o'clock. The excitement had sharpened my appetite. "My old friend," I said, "another case resolved, even if the outcome was not the one we expected. Shall we dine at Simpson's to celebrate the survival of our Great Queen, still and forever *Ind. Imp?*" adding with heavy irony, "and drink a toast to our absent friend Giles Gilchrist and his tracking skills for her survival."

Holmes reached for his ear flapped cap. "The Grand Cigar Divan it is!" he confirmed.

The *Maître d'hôtel* greeted Holmes with the respect more accorded to a Prime Minister. We threaded our way to a table with a fine view overlooking the bustling Strand. The Chef appeared, walking alongside a lesser mortal propelling a silver dinner wagon. Holmes ordered slices of beef carved from large joints, with a portion of fat. I chose the smoked salmon, at a price well beyond my usual range.

I was on the last spoonful of the Divan's famous treacle sponge dressed with Madagascan vanilla custard when Holmes asked, "Watson, the Old Sheffield plated Entrée dish at the back of your elbow. How did it get there?"

I lifted my arm. "I've no idea," I replied, staring at it. I summoned the waiter. He shook his head.

"Messieurs, I do not know," he replied. He reached for our empty dessert plates. As he turned away, he said in a plaintive tone, "Why would I serve an *entrée* dish at the *completion* of your meal?"

"Go ahead, Watson," Holmes ordered. "Lift the lid."

I did so to reveal a page torn from a notebook. On it was scribbled: "*As to Philip, do not imagine that his empire is everlastingly secured to him as a god.*"

"Gilchrist's handwriting," I exclaimed, "but what on Earth does it mean?"

"Demosthenes," Holmes replied, looking around the crowded restaurant. "From the First Philippic. I baited him too far. This singular episode has not reached its conclusion. He thirsts for revenge. This note tells us one thing for sure – he's *not* under guard a quarter-way to the Lesser Sunda Islands after all. He's escaped the clutches of the police."

"You suggest he's...?"

"...right here. Perhaps a waiter. Or what about the marquis behind us with the monocle? The only giant yellow-tongued lizards he's after are Holmes and Watson. And the *.50-95* Express is a very heavy cartridge indeed!"

The End

© Tim Symonds and Lesley Abdela 2018

MY THANKS TO -

All those many who have risen to the occasion when I have sought out clarity in subjects new to me, including the horse-racing world and early military aviation as in 'The Pegasus Affair'.

AND

First and always to Steve Emecz and his colleagues at MX Publishing (London). His and their indefatigable work on behalf of us authors has turned MX into the world's largest publisher of Sherlock Holmes' stories.

My partner Lesley Abdela in the deep English countryside without whose presence and help my novels and short stories would never have been written.

David Marcum in Maryville, Tennessee, whose keen eye and indefatigable energy as Editor has been one of the real pleasures in writing these stories.

Jeff Sobel in faraway California whose deep knowledge of firearms and explosives can be seen in several of my novels and some of these short stories.

Brian Belanger in Vermont for the cover of this book of my short stories who also did the wonderfully dramatic cover to my novel 'Sherlock Holmes And The Nine-Dragon Sigil'.

For more on Tim Symonds' short stories and five Sherlock Holmes novels see http://tim-symonds.co.uk

Also by Tim Symonds

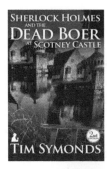 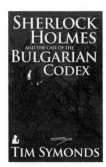 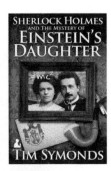

Sherlock Holmes And The Dead Boer at Scotney Castle

Sherlock Holmes And The Bulgarian Codex

Sherlock Holmes And The Mystery of Einstein's
Daughter

Sherlock Holmes And The Sword of Osman

Sherlock Holmes And The Nine-Dragon Sigil

MX Publishing

www.sherlockholmesbooks.com

MX Publishing is the world's largest specialist Sherlock Holmes publisher, with over a hundred titles and fifty authors creating the latest in Sherlock Holmes fiction and non-fiction.

From traditional short stories and novels to travel guides and quiz books, MX Publishing cater for all Holmes fans.

The collection includes leading titles such as *Benedict Cumberbatch In Transition* and *The Norwood Author* which won the 2011 Howlett Award (Sherlock Holmes Book of the Year).

MX Publishing also has one of the largest communities of Holmes fans on Facebook with regular contributions from dozens of authors.

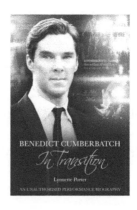

Also from MX Publishing

  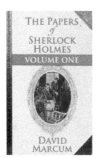

Our bestselling books are our short story collections;

'Lost Stories of Sherlock Holmes' , 'The Outstanding
Mysteries of Sherlock Holmes', The Papers of Sherlock
Holmes Volume 1 and 2, 'Untold Adventures of Sherlock
Holmes' (and the sequel 'Studies in Legacy) and 'Sherlock
Holmes in Pursuit', 'The Cotswold Werewolf and Other
Stories of Sherlock Holmes' – and many more......

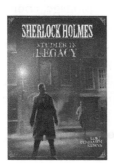  

www.sherlockholmesbooks.com

Also from MX Publishing

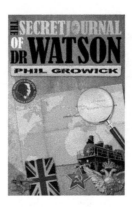

"Phil Growick's, 'The Secret Journal of Dr Watson', is an adventure which takes place in the latter part of Holmes and Watson's lives. They are entrusted by HM Government (although not officially) and the King no less to undertake a rescue mission to save the Romanovs, Russia's Royal family from a grisly end at the hand of the Bolsheviks. There is a wealth of detail in the story but not so much as would detract us from the enjoyment of the story. Espionage, counter-espionage, the ace of spies himself, double-agents, double-crossers...all these flit across the pages in a realistic and exciting way. All the characters are extremely well-drawn and Mr Growick, most importantly, does not falter with a very good ear for Holmesian dialogue indeed. Highly recommended. A five-star effort."
The Baker Street Society

www.sherlockholmesbooks.com

Also from MX Publishing

The Missing Authors Series

Sherlock Holmes and The Adventure of The Grinning Cat
Sherlock Holmes and The Nautilus Adventure
Sherlock Holmes and The Round Table Adventure

"Joseph Svec, III is brilliant in entwining two endearing and enduring classics of literature, blending the factual with the fantastical; the playful with the pensive; and the mischievous with the mysterious. We shall, all of us young and old, benefit with a cup of tea, a tranquil afternoon, and a copy of Sherlock Holmes, The Adventure of the Grinning Cat."
Amador County Holmes Hounds Sherlockian Society

www.sherlockholmesbooks.com

Also from MX Publishing

The American Literati Series

 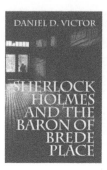 

The Final Page of Baker Street
The Baron of Brede Place
Seventeen Minutes To Baker Street

"The really amazing thing about this book is the author's ability
to call up the 'essence' of both the Baker Street 'digs' of
Holmes and Watson as well as that of the 'mean streets' of
Marlowe's Los Angeles. Although none of the action takes
place in either place, Holmes and Watson share a sense of
camaraderie and self-confidence in facing threats and problems
that also pervades many of the later tales in the Canon.
Following their conversations and banter is a return to
Edwardian England and its certainties and hope for the future.
This is definitely the world before The Great War."
Philip K Jones

www.sherlockholmesbooks.com

Also from MX Publishing

The Detective and The Woman Series

The Detective and The Woman
The Detective, The Woman and The Winking Tree
The Detective, The Woman and The Silent Hive

"The book is entertaining, puzzling and a lot of fun. I believe the author has hit on the only type of long-term relationship possible for Sherlock Holmes and Irene Adler. The details of the narrative only add force to the romantic defects we expect in both of them and their growth and development are truly marvelous to watch. This is not a love story. Instead, it is a coming-of-age tale starring two of our favorite characters."
Philip K Jones

www.sherlockholmesbooks.com

163